MARK DOWSON

RECOG₂NITION

HYPNO-XIA

PART 3

"*ReCo2gnition* is an intelligent, well-crafted thriller with great forward momentum, lots of intrigue and memorable characters."

—RADHA SPRATT, Editor of the South Asian Literature Festival's magazine and The Marlowe Society Journal

"What happens when Science Fiction meets science, art, philosophy, and architecture? Well, naturally, you get a compelling story! Dowson has outdone himself in this second book of the Recognition series. The action ramps up while still delivering insight all designed to help us of this time to avoid mistakes which will make the future wholly unlivable. Thought provoking and inspiring!"

—JIM ARROWOOD, Sci Fi Blogger, jimsscii.blogspot.com

"Science fact and science fiction collide in this eco-thriller from Mark Dowson. Two time travelers from 2112 return to the present day, one to assassinate a wind energy engineer, the other to rescue him—and perhaps save the planet!"

—DOUG PILLEY, Author of Tales from the Multiverse: Stories Beyond Your Imagination

"A convincing portrayal of a potentially dark future, a clear warning that our current lack of commitment and reckless environmental behaviour can destroy nature and end our dream of a prosperous future.

"The vision and conviction of the author is not only outstanding but serious. The shorty line is effective in exploring new thinking and even technical solutions.

"It is promising to see that the new generation is taking environmental challenges seriously and trying to spread the idea through story telling."

—MAHTAB FARSHCHI, Course Director, University of West London

"If you like crime, mystery and romance all wrapped up in a sci-fi thriller, this is for you. Mark has also introduced today's global concerns as a crucial theme, and if that isn't enough, he's cleverly focused on mental health too. You'll need to concentrate, but that's its magic. This, the middle of Mark's trilogy sets things up nicely for the third book finalé.

Once again it's a fast-paced read full of thought provoking science based drama with just a touch of sci-fi to embellish the storyline.

It's up to date making use of the Coronavirus and yet still manages to draw the reader into the future and the past.

You need to concentrate - but it's worth it."

"A great sequel from Mark Dowson to his first instalment of *ReCO2gnition*. Building on the enigmatic characters of the launch volume of *ReCO2gnition* the author maintains his pursuit of exploring big contemporary challenges to the human condition against the intriguing backdrop of futuristic science fiction. This time it is the pandemic. Another intriguing and enjoyable read."

"Sci-fi, ecosensitive, time-travelling thriller which alternates between the present and a post apocalyptic world where a leading scientific genius must be transported to the future to save humanity. Keeps you guessing to the end whether he will succeed or not."

"A great read. Time shifting and hi technology giving a vision of the 22nd Century if we let things continue as they are, not a pleasant vision of the future. Our thoughtful lead, Ben Richards leaves all the super hero stuff and the 22nd Century players. Very like a Greek mythical legend would go on a journey of discovery to save the future of the planet. The environmental issues of global warming are well discussed and the consequence of bad decisions clearly a warning for all readers. Each of the characters are well fleshed out and all the tech detail felt credible."

—ALASDAIR GIBSON, Sales Director, Mohn Media UK

"Creative Mark Dowson is at it again, drawing your mind into moments of imagery and situations that bring characters to life."

— ADRIENNE MAZZONE, President, TransMedia Group

"I read book 1 and couldn't wait for book 2. You won't be disappointed. Book 2 is even faster and more thrilling! You don't want to put the book down. Mark Dowson with his expertise on wind energy has created a Sci-Fi Thriller, no one else can! An incredible read that+ truly makes you think about our world."

—ANNA MARIE PELOSO, Internationally acclaimed Narrator of audiobooks, New Jersey, USA.

"Groundbreaking time travel concept that is original, revolutionary and has never been thought of before, in the world of science fiction. Mark Dowson uses a factual artefact as mystical form of timetravel. Fascinating!"

—KARTIK SPRATT, Director, Thames Consultancy Services.

"Doctor Richards is back and time travelling and mystery solving has never been so engaging. Ben Richards is pulled further into a future conspiracy...but has time ran out for him and us? A thoroughly entertaining read this ground breaking sequel picks up shortly after the original and looks even deeper into the millenia old mysteries of sator square,"

— CHRISTIAN GRIFFITHS, Sales Executive, Warwick Development, Liverpool

Part 1 Reviews

Review 1
By: inveterate_reader

"Oxygen Debt" is a really well-crafted piece. It is engaging, it is intriguing, and it has mysterious characters & a great pace. It actually keeps you hooked! The book gives strong Dan Brown vibes, touches art & history, keeping everything interesting. It is thought provoking, makes one think about the future of our planet & how our resources won't last forever. It shows a glimpse of our future which is quite bone chilling.

Review 2
By: twinslifeinpages

Recognition oxygen debt one is a book written in the science fiction genre. It seems to be a well-researched book and enlightens the reader with futuristic aspects as well as with climate and a touch of religion too! I really liked how the author built up the plot adding touches of mystery, thrill as well as interesting characters.

Review 3
By: its.haadi

I loved the historical references and the setting in Italy was such a smart choice by the author. The side character of Rossini was easily lovable from the start. And the cliffhanger at the end was pure "knife in my heart"

Review 4
By: sparkling_chapters

This book certainly got me into sci-fi. Particularly when I am right now aiming for diverse genres. It is a sci-fi thriller novel with fascinating perception of history science and religion. The best part of the characters, they were well interpreted and amazingly developed. The twist and turns keep you at the edge. And the way it ended on the cliffhanger just craved me to pick up the second book.

Review 5
By: khulogophile_reads

Book 1: Oxygen Debt: The book is a suspenseful science fiction novel. It was the author's first book. The book is set in the year 2112, and it is all about technology. The earth is in peril, but despite such advanced technology, it is still unable to make life easier for the earth. Dr. Ben Richards, who comes up with a novel approach to use wind power to alter the course of human history. The book has a lot of useful information. It not only entertains the reader but also provides a wealth of technological knowledge. The characters, especially Grazia and Merisi, are strange and intriguing. Another astonishing thing I discovered was that the author covered a wide range of topics throughout the book, including physics, history, and philosophy.

Part 2 Reviews

Review 1
By: inveterate_reader

"Co-Anda 19 Vaccine" is really fast paced. The first book creates the framework while the second book tells the story, the 'happenings'. It's gripping. It has some beautiful artwork & goes in detail while elaborating the art & its meaning. There's quite some action in the book. The characters are on a run. There are explanations of the future world working, how it all came to that. It talks about corruption, capitalism & human's greed that ultimately causes all the problems.

Review 2
By: twinslifeinpages

Recognition- CO-ANDA 19 vaccine in this book is the second book of the recognition series and here things start to fall in line, and everything makes much more sense. I must say that the author has cleverly written this book with a fast pace that doesn't let the reader feel bored.

Review 3
By: its.haadi

I particularly enjoyed the hint of the ongoing "COVID-19 Pandemic". However, the suspense would still continue in Part 3 which I'm looking forward to!

Review 4
By: sparkling_chapters

This part has more prolonging information than in part one and frankly it was more sensational. But again, there was a cliffhanger there. I adore how the author wraps all the topics while twirling them into beautiful mystery.

Review 5
By: khulogophile_reads

The plot thickens as it progresses, incorporating time travel, history, science, environmental activism, and much more. That's why it's important to read the first part of the book because the incidents and events of the story continue from part 1 of the series, which includes some background information. In this scene, Dr. Richard is in the hospital and has lost his memory; on the other hand, Feng is eager to study every move Dr. Richard makes. Part 2 of the series will take you back to Dr. Richard's journey and the problems he meets throughout the novel. Because of the book's atmosphere and plot, part 2 is equally as fascinating and intriguing as part 1.

Collective Reviews

Review 1
By: thebookgeek1

The recognition trilogy is dystopian sci-fi, and these books not only entertain the readers but educate them as well. The stories are progressive, and the curiosity will keep you on your toes. The characters are very intelligently developed. Both books are full of knowledge, twists and turns, thrill, and action. They consist of thought-provoking content and factual details. All in all, very well researched with lots of suspense and action.

Review 2
By: fableyll

This series touches important events like covid, tsunamis and other natural occurrences that we are currently facing, and the author uses them as a wakeup call that our planet is heading towards a similar situation unless we do something about it. Nonetheless, the books were action packed, the ending was intriguing and I'm eager for the next part.

Review 3
By: mybookishcorner10

Both books are quick and easy with very simple vocabulary that can be understood by everyone. Author has kept everything to the point and made it interesting. Entertaining and knowledgeable! The recognition series is my most favourite and I cannot wait for the last part because I know it's going to be the most interesting and exciting of all. Desperately waiting!!

Review 4
By: bookishfaery

Really made me think about how my decisions today will affect the earth in a hundred or so years. If anything, this book made me a cautious of actions for the prevention of the damage of my surroundings.

Review 5
By: its.haadi

Dowson's trilogy comprising of time travel, secret codes themed elements in a written format was certainly a worthwhile experience to read. The little technical details during the plot all showed his knowledge of "Wind Energy" that he so cleverly penned down.

Review 1
By: reading.addict10

Ok so this is the final part of recognition and I waited for quite some time for this. I'm so glad that it is out and I got the chance to read it. This part is so advanced and a bit different from the other 2 parts. 3rd part has so many details and answers of questions that I was unable to get in the first 2 parts. The author has a very unique writing style, he has revealed so many things slowly and gradually while incorporating all the details in the description. Finally I found out about Dr Richards end and how he was fearless and powerful. His personality is literally my fav. He's such an innocent yet strong protagonist. I love this trilogy and I highly highly recommend it to everyone out there!

Review 2
By: bookishfaery

Like any series, Recognition Hypno-xia Part 3 picks up right where we left off. AND THANK GOODNESS I GOT MY ANSWERS. The author has a very intellectual style of writing that had me intrigued at every page turn. Honestly, the amount of research that must have gone into this book deserves 'Recognition' (pun intended). Dr Richards has to be one of my favorite smart scientist protagonist. He's really trying his best. Overall, definitely worth the read. Kept me on my toes. Endings are always worth it!

Review 3
By: wanderingreads_byfati

Recognition Hypno-Xia is last part of this series. So finally this trilogy is completed and this part is different from last two parts and how the things changed, and how the author reveals all the things which really intrigued my interest. And how can I forget Dr

Richard who is the most powerful and smart scientist. Overall this sci-fi trilogy is a good read, I enjoyed it and it's a different genre for me. If you are Sci-Fi lover you should must give it a try!

Review 4
By: samsbookreviews_

One of my favorite scifi series came to an end. And gosh what a brilliant way to conclude this series. This book was exhilarating, it picked up from where the second book ended. I commend the author for his extensive research and also for conveying his research to us readers in such an entertaining manner. It bombards you with loads of information but you won't get irritated at all. I thought this book only dealt with technology and global warming but it is so much more than that. It deals with grief and traumas as well. This book proved that no AI no matter how capable can ever replace humanity. Ben Richards is hands down one of my favorite scientist in a book world. He is intelligent, passionate, smart and softy at heart as well. It was an amazing experience seeing his while journey throughout this series. And the ending sequence was penned down brilliantly. All the loose ends were tied in a brilliant manner. An unexpected ending it had. A must read for all the thrill loving scifi readers.

Review 5
By: aabdarsworld

Firstly I want to talk about the cover that is so intriguing and enthralling as well. The title is self-explanatory, how? You come to know when you read it. It's a fast pace sci-fi, full of engrossing scenes that going to give chills down to your spine. I love the way the writer uses metaphors to explain a lot of the harsh realities of our tech-obsess society. Climate change is so real and we have to save our world on our own. I'm a graduate of psychology and I know the concepts of Gestalt psychology and alter ego, that's why I love this part of the series more because the writer penned down amazingly and because of my education in psychology, I love all the references the writer jotted down. The book ends in a thought-provoking way and honestly, I didn't expect this end. I adore this book, I really do. And I wish that it made to Netflix one day. Highly recommended to each and every one out there.

Review 6
By: thebookbutterflysquotage

With the release of the 3rd book, the Recognition trilogy comes an end & what a perfect way to conclude this impressive, action-packed, exhilarating and thought-provoking adventure. The story resumes from where it was left off hanging on a cliffhanger in the 2nd book and all the answers we've been craving until now are finally offered to us. This book is an even blend of thrilling sci-fi, intriguing & awe-inspiring research, well-pondered over creative thoughts, with a pinch of romance thrown in. Throughout the book, the author stresses the importance of following a correct philosophy and how the salvation of the world relies on more creative visionary leaders + creative thinkers rather than motivational speakers. The book is filled with metaphors, themes & elements with hidden meanings and symbolism and I loved highlighting all the quote-worthy lines. The way the author draws parallels between the element of time travel & spiritual journey/development and shape-shifting with trauma, deserves all the praise it can possibly get. I had such a great time reading Dr Richards' interesting thoughts & astounding reflections and I can happily declare that it was in fact my favourite part of the whole thrilling adventure.

Review 7
By: hercrazybooksta

Okay, so while I'm not really a sci-fi kind of a person (mostly because I'm dumb and can't grasp the concepts), as soon I finished book 2, I needed the next book in my life, I needed to know what happens next. This one had some technical explanations, too, and it's not the kind of a book you can genuinely enjoy if you're not familiar with some scientific concepts. I could understand some, but it honestly bored me too sometimes, and I needed to get on with the story again, to know what happens. Which is to say, it was engaging in a way that you immediately wanted to know what happens to the characters. As a plot, it was an enjoyable read. And oh that plot twist at the end! The last chapter... I'll try not to give much away but I was truly shocked. It's hard for me to be shocked by plot twists, but this one caught me completely off-guard. I never saw that coming. Once again, if you have some grasp around science, and you enjoy dystopian stories where there's an important message, this book is for you. I personally liked the overall message the author has tried to convey to mankind.

Review 8
By: weebreader

Hypno-Xia is the third book in the splendid Sci-fi Recognition series. Some secrets are revealed in this book, Ben Richards slowly gets over his trauma and we get to see his character development and this book takes some other crazy turns. This book was surprisingly good and my favorite one from the series. I liked the turn of events in here and the perfect description of the wretched future world with extreme global warming, depressed people, the arrival of many viral diseases and androids taking over who had no emotions which would lead to an unimaginable destruction of the whole world. I enjoyed this part a lot and I am happy with the way it ended.

Review 9
By: biblolater

This is the last book of one of my fav trilogy, second book was ended on a cliffhanger, I was very curious when I finished the second book but I'm now at peace coz I have all answers now. The author has done a marvelous job, the plot was insanely good, I loved it and it's a must read if you love thrill. Here is one of my fav line from this book: "The Therapy is designed to take you to places to which you would not normally be able to go".

Review 10
By: its_b.e.l.l.e

A futuristic dystopian sci-fi thriller with enhanced humans and android doppelgangers that focuses on a twenty-first-century inventor Dr Ben Richards, who created a way to harness wind power, clean and renewable energy. He could have changed the course of humanity if he hadn't died under mysterious circumstances.

The UNA determines that keeping Richards alive in 2017 is key to saving the world from becoming a nuclear wasteland. Meanwhile, GIATCOM is using every method at its disposal, including enhanced humans and android doppelgangers, to thwart that effort and capture Richards for its own purposes, setting up an epic battle between future powers in the past. After an action-packed book one and book two, I was excited to read the last book of the trilogy. The way the story was taken was really interesting. It was a twist I did not see coming. It was a pleasant surprise. The consistency in the amount of information was refreshing... like the author delivered what was expected. There were a few aspects of the ending that felt bizarre while reading but in the end, I enjoyed the read.

Review 11
By: danthewandererboy

This is the final part of book series. The story has been set in the dystopian world where in year 2112, United Nation Authority is trying to save the world from GIATCOM and Dr Ben Richards is the only solution for them but he died years ago so they have to time travel in 2017 and convince Dr Richards for help. In the third book, the battle between humans and machines continues. The story as always like the previous books has written in an engaging style with the knowledge and references of past events. The story is the mixture of historical events and their use in modern world. The cover of the book is also a cherry on the cake. The use of psychology in this series is amazing and I like how all the concepts used throughout this series are real and most of the things are possible in real world. Totally recommended.

Review 12
By: mybookishcorner10

Last part is one hell of a read. So much happens in it so many ups and downs. I could hardly out it down to grasp everything. Finally all the doubts are cleared and answers are given in this part. There are so many surprises in this part revealing so many secrets and hidden things that we didn't notice before. Finally the protagonist Dr Richards proves himself strong and worthy of all the struggles. There's a secret surprise about Feng but you will have to read this book to find out. Amazing plot and intriguing storyline. I'm amazing, shocked and satisfied. Hightail recommend this trilogy. Don't miss out!

Review 13
By: nehajamal_

The third book picks up right where we left off the second, with Dr Ben Richards opening his eyes after the fight with Shui Feng to find himself safe and the damage repaired. Following that, an android showed him a detailed presentation about history and told him about the consequences the world might face in the future. They then prepared him for his mission and sent him back in time, where he completed it. The section that follows is truly remarkable, with the reader feeling as if the author has played an unexpected game with their minds. As revealed in the last chapter, the entire previous reading was about the treatment of Xia Feng's ptsd, which was been cured by Dr Westcroft. All about her trauma of witnessing her mother's death in front of her eyes, as well as the visions she has for her future, in which her mind travels through all the scenarios with the characters she desires. A therapy session in which a patient is hypnotised and lives out everything in their mind as a story. The author did discuss the effects of climate change and its disastrous consequences, global warming, wind energy, and turbines. And, most notably, Dowson revealed about the recognition very deeply and powerfully with the character of Ben, who was the true survivor as he desired to be recognised by the world. As the author wrote "Your own concept of time travel is your own spiritual journey, to enable you to find your own belief, identity and vision." And that's the real time when you realize that why this book series called Recognition. What an exceptional book series it is! Well done!

Review 14
By: fableyll

This is the final book in the recognition series set in the future where the planet is on the brink of collapse and the people are desperate enough to send someone back in time to save Ben Richards whose invention can save the planet's health. However, there are forces working against this mission for their own power hungry agenda.

Without spoiling it much, Hypno-xia kicks off with Ben waking up from a coma, 7 weeks after his encounter with Shui Feng. After this, the events of the book are well-paced and exciting and I liked the way the book ended. You can check out my review for the first two books as well.

Review 15
By: the_busy_book_bandit

The book follows the story of a 21st century inventor Dr Ben Richards who is sent through a time portal to the year 2112 to witness the demise of humankind. The author describes with great shrewdness the adverse effects of Climatic change and increasing mental health issues that become the main reason of the fall of humankind. Interestingly, author presents a theory about COVID-19 being a manmade pandemic to improve economic growth within the global healthcare sector. Also in future CRISPR technology is used with Artificial Intelligence to enhance human beings' capability to survive climatic change. In short, in the year 2112, humans become half android called humanoids. This book is a fight between good and evil, between UNA and GIATCOM (two opposing organizations). The ending was perfect! If you are sci-fi and futuristic dystopian fan, you should check out this book. The special thing about it is that it is very informative but doesn't bore you at all and provides a great insight into what our future would look like if we continue destroying the atmosphere.

Review 16
By: thecrafty.readerbee

This is third book of Recognition Trilogy that is a dystopian fiction. I am not a huge fan of sci-fi books because it is hard for me grasp some concepts, but this one was a hella interesting read. As the previous book ended with a cliffhanger so I was really very excited to read this one. The story is set in 2112, it revolves around the harms caused by excessive use of technology in long term. GIATCOM is a powerful organization that is on its way to destroy society. The scientist, as well as the hero, Dr Ben Richards, had created a way to use wind power, a clean and renewable energy that could have changed the course of humanity but unfortunately he died a long time ago. The UNA decides to go back in time and save Dr Richards to protect this world and prevent it from becoming a nuclear wasteland. On the other hand, GIATCOM is using every method to use Dr Ben Richards for its own purposes and evil plans. Some idea were still hard for me to understand, but I also enjoyed reading this one as it was a new experience for me.

Review 17
By: bookishnerd9

Okay, Ending was Epic! Perfect & satisfying. This trilogy gave me TOTALLY DIFFERENT Experience. The ideas shared by the author. The efforts of author writing this trilogy is clearly showed here. I've come to know the main theme of this book besides the innovative ideas, masterminded Plot is that it showed the How greater importance our mental health have in our life. How much it matters, how it affects our creativity and all aspects of our life. How greater the impact it has. I am really really astonished by the way of author's writing which conveyed such deep topics in a beautiful way. One of my fav lines of the author is "Recognising that it is not our own individual behaviour, but the circumstance of an event that creates who we become. We are who we are from the circumstance that is created around us, with us in it". Which is actually Trauma.

Review 18
By: pearlescentpages

Hypno-xia is the final book in the Reco2gnition trilogy. This book doesn't only focus on futuristic technology and environment awareness, but it also deals with human emotions, trauma, and the affect these have on our daily lives in the most minor of things. I enjoyed this final book way more than the first two books! It had a clear message and it answered all of the questions we had in the first and second book. Dr Ben Richards' fight wasn't only against GIATCOM, it was against his personal traumas too. I absolutely loved how the author depicted Richards' internal struggles and his realizations. Due to this, our mc didn't feel like a character, he felt real. His actions, his thought process, his reactions, everything felt relatable and REAL. Secondly, damn I loved the 180° shift at the end! I totally wasn't expecting the ending. But it was well-concluded. Like always, I really enjoyed how the author researched everything so perfectly. I feel like he himself came from the future to warn us with how realistic these books were! We should all realize the role we play in taking care of our planet, and make an effort to protect it.

Review 19
By: Anonymous

The 2nd part of this series left us on a cliffhanger but the 3rd and the last part picks up where it left off and makes sure we get all our answers. Our favorite, Dr Ben Richards tries his best to keep humanity alive and safe. The best thing about this book was the message it relayed that no matter how advanced. AI gets, it can never replace humanity. Oh, and the end! OMG! If you read all three books together, I kid you not you will literally go WHATTTTTT? By the time you reach its end. The plot twist is mind-bogglingly and jaw-droopingly good. All in all, I loved the series, especially how the plot unrolled. Although the technical parts did get boring at times, especially with this part. But overall, I loved how the author has weaved technicalities into prose.

Review 20
By: khulogophile_reads

This is the last and third book of Reco2gnition. The most awaited book is finally here and it's as enjoyable as the previous parts. The story is all about dystopian world 2112 and it's facing a disastrous change and UNA is doing the best to save the world. One of the main characters of course Dr Richards who is trying to make a renewable energy that will change the earth so that it can be saved. If you love sci-fi then you should read this unique and awesome series. For me it was a different read than you usually do. The author did an amazing job with writing style and with this book, so much relatable regarding our current lifestyle. All fun character is with Dr Richards how smart and strong with intelligence. So glad that I got the opportunity to read this trilogy and good luck to the author for the future.

Review 21
By: zee_verse6

This is the last part of Recognition Trilogy resuming the story in second part. And as I told y'all earlier I'm a big sci-fi fan so this last part wasn't less than a treat for me, I've been waiting for this to know either Dr Ben Richards our protagonist will be succeeded or failed to save the humanity! So yes he did and fought against the Giatcom. The story begins with Dr Richards in 2112 where he got to know the disastrous situation humanity is facing because of excessive technology. The plot twist is just amazing I mean how did the author even imagined that!! I loved the absolutely thought provoking ending. The story is fast paced, intriguing and flow beautifully so I didn't feel bored at all. Highly recommended to everyone interested in Future of Tech and humanity.

Review 22
By: thebookgeek1

Reco2gnition Hypno-xia is the third installment in the trilogy and I can safely say that this part is a rollercoaster ride. There are multiple plot twists in it and this part continues from where the second part ended. It answers so many unanswered questions from the first two parts, puts all the pieces together and of course, the whole storyline makes sense. There are extensive details and explanations in this part with a few vibrant illustrations to make it more understandable and give us a clear insight into the future as well as the damage caused by humans. The author brings attention to some serious and thought-provoking aspects related to our environment and earth in general. Time travel (comparison between present and future) and ecology are two excellent topics that are discussed in this book, which forces us to think about the choices we make. The story is thrilling and equally informative, fast-paced with intelligible language. Mark Dowson has a very unique and simple writing style which makes it easy to understand the whole concept. I highly recommend this book.

Review 23
By: arshima_gul

RECO2GNITION is a series of 3 books, I've read all of them and the 3rd one is just another fabulous, fantastic and unique piece by the author. The previous two books talked about artificial intelligence, viruses, our planet it's environment and humanoids and were honestly, "SCI-FIC. THRILLER THAT IS FACTFULL, A FACT BASED FICTION BOOK" This book, the third part of recognition series, is about the DESTRUCTION DONE BY THE MASSIVE TECHNOLOGY. One thing that I loved about all of these three books, the writing style is so impressive, even the chapter titles are so accurate and complimenting with each other... like something you can sense by turning pages is reality. All of the books of this series are masterpieces, by every turning page you'll get to know how much research is done before writing it! TWO THINGS THAT THIS BOOK HIGHLY SUGGESTS! That the book is based on a topic, almost no one bothers to write on. It is new yet innovative to read something factual on such thing (technology) which is a massive part of our life. The book suggests the strong imagination of the author. Who have created a whole world of "FACT BASED FICTION"

Review 24
By: its.haadi

About the Book: The book is the final part of the "RECO2GNITION Trilogy" where the world has been plunged into dystopia in the year 2112 and efforts are made to reset the course of mankind from this dark fate. This is my third experience reading the "Reco2gnition Trilogy", I became a fan from the start and since Co Anda-19 Vaccine had been waiting for the ending. Don't know about anyone else but I decided to go on a binge read to really get into the zone and it indeed has paid out to be worthwhile. Hypno-Xia used a slightly different literature style than its predecessors with much more attention to technical details yet still maintaining the fun. Yep, the cliffhanger sure had its theme I mean who knew the protagonist would turn out to be so clever and the thriller/romance portrayal of events was something I was hoping to get a taste of from the start. Having done a cover reveal recently I maintain that this particular trilogy can be adopted into a spectacular sci-fi film or series. Verdict: Apart from being a Sci-Fi thriller, RECO2GNITION has in itself a dire message on climate change and global warming for the people of the 21st Century & I believe that's the perfect ending to an epic series. Hence this particular trilogy falls into my recommendations. My journey reading Mark Dowson's works had been quite an exciting one.

Review 25
By: Anonymous

A fantastic book with amazing storyline. I must say this is the best one among all three books because this one has so many plot twists which kept me on my toes. I was hooked and I'm not even exaggerating! I'm glad that I read the last part as it answered so many questions I had regarding Dr Richards, Grazia and Feng. There's a big secret reveal regarding Feng and I was so intrigued and surprised. I'm so happy and satisfied with the ending except one thing: Grazia and Dr Richards love life. I mean come on, they should've gotten together for a little bit. But it's alright I'm glad that everything that happened, happened. Super engaging and intriguing! Absolutely recommended!

Review 26
By: book_with_girl

This is the third instalment of The Recognition series. And this book changed my all imaginations of this series literally. I was eagerly waiting for this book and this book put an end to the recognition series and my imagination. I was curious because the second book ended in such a way that I was eagerly wanting to know what will happen. And now I have all the answers. Really what an amazing and unique plot.
The most surprising was its end and also a big surprise about Feng(I'm not telling).
You have to read it to know.
Precisely I was amazed reading this series which has lots of ups and downs really...
Amazing plot, storytelling everything...

RECO₂GNITION:
Hypno - xia
Part 3

by Mark Dowson

ISBN 978-1-9168957-5-1

Published by

 Abstract2Construct Limited

38 Wenning Lane,
Emerson Valley,
Milton Keynes,
England
MK42JF
www.markdowsonauthor.com

Mark Dowson

RECOG$_2$NITION

HYPNO-XIA

PART 3

"REALITY IS MASKED BY ILLUSIONS"

FOREWORD

The internet is an amazing tool. Without it, I would probably never have learned about the first book in the series, ReCO2gnition: Oxygen Debt Part I, leading to my relationship with author Mark Dowson.

Mark contacted me through email asking if I would be interested in reading his first book. He included a description of the book and it hooked me as something I would enjoy. Enjoy was an understatement! I was amazed at what I read for two reasons. First was the depth of the story, and second, because of the wide variety of subjects Mark included in his tale. I love the characters and their development, as well as including the subjects of science, history, mystery, art, and mythology.

Mark and I have kept in contact over the past year through instant messaging and email, and I have witnessed his triumphs and his struggles in the production and marketing of his work. Writing is hard, but publishing, marketing, and creating a brand is even more difficult and frustrating. Mark has made it his mission to bring his dream to life, no matter the obstacles, both personal and professional, and try to make the future a better place for our children and grandchildren.

It is for that reason I admire Mark and have invested time and resources in bringing this project to life.

One of the overarching concerns put forth in the ReCO2gnition series? For me, the genuine concern of global climate change and its causes is at the forefront. Humanity is gluttonous in how we depend on limited resources to make our lives comfortable. We depend on limited resources to maintain and improve the lifestyle we have become accustomed to since the beginning of the Industrial Revolution. As a result, mining, drilling, and other methods to extract energy from our planet leave vast amounts of land scarred. We put tons of greenhouse gasses into the atmosphere and the evidence is clear there is change. Glacial ice is disappearing at an alarming rate, causing a rise in sea levels. Scientists project the future will differ greatly from what we see now, and it isn't good.

Change is hard, and it isn't made any easier by those who profit from conventional forms of energy production. While clear evidence of climate change presents itself all over the world, those who profit spend vast amounts of money to discount the mounting evidence, and they seem to be very effective in their efforts.

One of the themes in Mark's book is developing renewable and sustainable ways of producing energy to cut our dependence on limited resources to keep our planet clean while still enjoying a comfortable lifestyle. The idea of using spaces, such as stadiums that are only used a few times a month, to mount wind generators not only to produce energy for the use of the facility but also for the surrounding community, seems a valid solution. Yes, it will require a significant investment by the stadium owners, but I think it may be at least a step in the right direction.

The clock is ticking, and time is running out. It is past time to take global climate change seriously, or the future may be at risk. I feel sad when I look at my kids and their children and want to apologize, in advance, for what my generation has done to leave them to clean up the mess we are and have been making over the decades since I was born, and before.

I am honored that Mark has asked me to write this foreword to the third book in his series. I am equally ecstatic to have been able to play a small part in helping bring Mark's work to light as an editor. It is my hope that there will also be future opportunities for him and me to collaborate on future projects.

Mark Dowson adds his voice to a chorus of scientists and authors with an important message to the future, and I have enjoyed being a part of his efforts.

Dear reader, if this is your first venture into the ReCO2gnition series, I urge you to set this aside and read the first two volumes before continuing to get a complete picture of the world the author has created. Oh, and watch out for the plot twist at the end of this saga! It's brilliant!

Jim Arrowood
Blogger, Podcaster, Writer, and Science Enthusiast
Kearney, Nebraska, USA

PROLOGUE

A bright light pierced the darkness.
It awakened my soul.
It swung left – then right. It blinded me for a moment.
Then it went out to sea. Always searching. And still the blades turned.
A pale form bobbed up and down.
Lifeless.

****

I lay motionless. Nothing moved but the blades.
I loved the blades.
The blades were always there.
"Let her go," said a voice, out of sight.
"Let her go."
But who am I?
I am a man. I am a woman. I am many people. I change like the wind. I am shapeless. I see everything.
Who will I be when I awaken?

CHAPTER 1

STILL WATERS RUN DEEP

en Richards became aware of a gentle purring sound as he regained consciousness. Instinctively he related it to a machine of some kind – but it was a relaxing and peaceful sound, which appeared to complement the darkness that surrounded him. He felt completely at ease. For the time being his mind was free of all thoughts, and he saw and felt nothing. He could hear nothing, except the abstract and unidentified murmuring of the machine.

Then a voice returned him to reality, and to some basic level of awareness: "Dr Richards. Can you hear me?"

All of a sudden true consciousness returned. He remembered who he was, and he remembered his mission – and then he was reminded of the horror of what had taken place at the encampment... and - his legs!

He opened his eyes, and in the same instant tried to sit up – but found that he had been firmly secured in a horizontal position. The same voice – a woman's voice – reassured him: "Please do not try to get up, Dr Richards. You are safe now. You have been in an induced coma for seven weeks. We are bringing you back. Please be patient."

Richards looked into the eyes of the woman who was leaning over him with an expression that was unsmiling, yet calm and unthreatening. Her face was pale, and he noticed how her eyebrows were thin, but perfectly formed. He could not make out the colour of her eyes, as her head was partially silhouetted against the pure white of the panel light on the ceiling, but he was struck by the largeness of her irises. She was wearing a powder blue uniform which was unmistakably medical, rather than military in nature, which reassured Richards enough to enable him to relax. In an instant he was reminded of the horrendous injuries that Shui Feng had inflicted on him, and so instinctively raised his head to look down at his legs. The woman instantly read his thoughts: "Don't worry Doctor. You have new legs."

Richards looked at her with a combination of amazement and horror.

"You mean that you have replaced them with prosthetic legs?" he exclaimed.

"No... No!" replied the woman, clearly unfamiliar with the term 'prosthetic.' "No, they are legs. Feel!" she said, squeezing Richards' left thigh gently.

To his utter astonishment, Richards felt the touch of her hand as if the incident at the encampment had never happened.

"But – but my legs. They were so badly damaged!"

"Yes, and these are new ones. The rigid structure – that's equivalent to what used to be the bones in your legs – has been manufactured from cardonium, a material that you will not be familiar with. Basically, it is a material that mimics the properties of bone, except that it does not break or fracture. All muscles in your newly formed legs are also made up of an artificial material – the same carbon fibre material that is used to create androids – but the skin is your own. Your new Achilles tendons are made up of graphene, which has a tensile property and elasticity that far surpasses the strength and flexibility of a human's natural tendon fibres."

Richards' eyes opened wide at this suggestion.

"We removed your damaged limbs, and now your skin has grown back over the new structures. It's a very simple process

– all that is required is to stimulate the right stem cells. It takes about five weeks for an entire limb, but you will find that your new legs look exactly as they did before. Your DNA takes care of that."

Richards flexed both ankles, and then his knees – as far as the restraints would let him, and sure enough everything felt just as it had done before.

"Your nervous system has also repaired itself, so your new limbs will do exactly what your brain tells them to. But it might take a little while for you to get used to them, as they are far more powerful than your old legs, and every tendon and sinew is stronger and more flexible. It will take some practice before you are able to use them properly."

"And are there any other differences?" asked Richards. "There are a few. The renewed portion of your nervous system works at about eighty percent of its former efficiency, and so reaction time will be slightly slower, but that is not as critical as it would have been if we had replaced your hands. You will also find that the new legs are colder to the touch, as there is much less blood circulating around them – but they will never get tired, and once you are used to them, you will be able to run three times as fast as you could before. It will take some getting used to, and a little training – but I am here to help you with that."

"In fact, I think it is time that I introduced myself," she said with a smile. "My name is Argonne. I will not bore you with the details of my physical development, but I think you will consider me to be about half human and half android."

"So, which bits of you are human?" asked Richards – and then immediately regretted asking the question, as he reflected on what the true answer might be.

"Well, I certainly possess enough human sensibilities to be offended by such rude questions," replied Argonne, with mock indignation. Richards blushed slightly. "What you need to know," she continued, "is that I have been developed as a medical technician. My specialist function is the rehabilitation of humans after limb replacement."

"I am also here to offer you some counselling, as I am sure that you must have many questions that you would like answered."

"... like 'where am I?' and 'what on earth happened to me?'... you say that it was seven weeks ago?!" interjected Richards. "Yes, and you are lucky to be here, Dr Richards. Not only did you survive a nuclear explosion, but you also survived a close encounter with the notorious Shui Feng. Not many people meet him and survive. He is undoubtedly programmed to kill his target first, and then attend to any other objectives he might have afterwards, so we were surprised that there was anything left of you to repair."

"Yet, I have been assailed by this character a couple of times, now," said Richards, thoughtfully, "and he has had any number of opportunities to kill me..."

"Really? That's interesting," replied Argonne, who was not aware of Richards' encounters with Feng in 21st Century Italy.

"So, what happened to this... android? Did he escape with the drawings?" asked Richards.

"Yes, I'm afraid he did – and he terminated two of our android guards when making his escape. They were the ones who gave chase to him, whilst Chief of Police Michael Sitefinder attended to your wound. All of our personnel are trained in First Aid."

"'First Aid?" repeated Richards, with incredulity. He had previously associated the term with minor cuts and wasp stings.

"...Michael knew exactly what to do. He sedated you and stopped the bleeding until you and the other survivors of the explosion could be evacuated. You are very important to us, Dr Richards."

"And so... where am I now?"

"In Melbourne. Back at the UNA Headquarters. It's one of the last safe places left on this planet."

"And Feng?"

"We don't know. It is likely that he will have returned to your time once again. GIATCOM has the technology to send him to any point in the past, now – and now they know exactly where to send him, and at what point in time."

Richards tried to imagine what damage Shui Feng might have done, once back in 2017.

"But – he could have been up to all kinds of things over the past seven weeks," he exclaimed. "You need to send me back there immediately. I need to find Merisi and warn him!"

Suddenly, the thought of Merisi brought to mind someone else that meant a great deal to him. Someone whose safety he feared for – Grazia! If the person he thought was Grazia was in fact Shui Feng, then where was she? What could have happened to her? He was about to raise the question with Argonne, but the Class 655 Enhanced Human had already placed a reassuring hand on his shoulder and was addressing his concern for Merisi.

"Don't worry. Merisi has already been informed – and we have been keeping him up to date with the progress of your recovery. He is already on full alert for any sign of Shui Feng – and he has received orders to terminate him on sight."

"We will return you to your own time soon enough once you are fully recovered. The beauty of being able to travel through time is that there is no need for us to rush. We can certainly ensure that you arrive in your present before Shui Feng gets there. If, as we suspect, Feng has returned to the 21st Century, then it is to our advantage that we are able to move second. Alternatively, we can send you back to a time after Merisi has eliminated Feng. That will be far safer for you. We'll wait to receive information from Merisi. However, it is difficult to predict whether sending you back before Merisi's inevitable confrontation with Feng could be benefitted by your presence being there."

"In what way?"

"Well Doctor, you could in fact intervene to help Merisi. We can't afford to take any chances with Merisi not being able to eliminate Feng, and the more support he can have, the better. Therefore, I would rather send you back before we get news of Merisi's confrontation with Feng, and at a convention where all the world leaders are to meet with a strong chance of Feng turning up. That way you will not only be able to prevent Feng from winning his own investment in your ideas he has stolen, but you get a chance to win investment for your own ideas and help Merisi terminate Feng's existence."

Richards reflected for a moment, trying to understand the new possibilities and opportunities that time travel presented.

"But before we send you back to 2017," continued Argonne, "there are many things that you should learn about. Many things have happened since then!"

Ben Richards relaxed on a sofa, wearing some casual garments, courtesy of the UNA that Argonne had provided for him. They were both seated in what appeared to be a large, frameless conservatory, which looked out on a paved patio, with spacious, formal gardens beyond. The vegetation was unmistakably tropical – palm trees and shrubs with dark green leaves and brightly coloured blooms, and lush, green lawns that were obviously reliant on a fairly comprehensive irrigation system.

The hazy scene beneath a cloudless, blue Australian sky was extremely inviting, yet the spacious glass room was fully enclosed. "It's fifty-one degrees centigrade outside," Argonne had explained, when Richards had suggested taking a stroll in the garden. "No human being would survive in this city in the summer months, without air conditioning."

Argonne had been supervising her patient's recuperation from the induced coma and the major surgical procedures that he had undergone with the utmost diligence and attention to detail. Every stage of the procedure had been carried out in a strict order of priority. First, she gave Richards something to drink – a precise measure of fluid, to achieve the desired level of hydration. Then she produced a meal, from what Ben thought looked rather like a microwave oven. It was food that might have been served at any restaurant that Ben had frequented during his lifetime – pasta and chicken, in a sort of cheese and ham sauce. He wondered whether the UNA had carried out research in order to provide him with 21st Century cuisine. In any event, such was his hunger that he gratefully devoured the offering, without pausing to ask questions about the food's origins.

Then, there was a carefully planned session of physiotherapy, to enable Richards to get accustomed to his new limbs, and exercises to strengthen his back and his arms, which had been inactive for seven weeks.

Throughout this first day of recovery, Argonne had patiently answered the majority of the scientist and engineer's questions about the various technologies that he came across – although most of the technical details that she reeled off were well beyond even his understanding. She also told him a great deal about what was known of Shui Feng, and about the life of his friend Merisi. But to his dismay, there was nothing that Argonne could tell Ben about the fate or the whereabouts of Grazia.

One line of questioning that Argonne avoided responding directly to however, was anything connected with the politics or history of the world over the previous one hundred years. Any such query was met with the blanket reply of: "Be patient. All will be revealed later."

It was early evening before Richards' curiosity was satisfied. After a further, precisely drilled set of walking and balancing exercises – which he performed remarkably well and intuitively – Argonne led Richards away from the still bright sunlight, into a partially darkened room. As soon as they were both seated, and without a word of introduction from Argonne, a three-dimensional image both filled and illuminated the room.

Initially, Richards sat back and marvelled at what was to him the most astonishing and immersive cinematic experience of his life – but it soon became clear that the presentation that had been prepared for him was a factual account of the harrowing events that had taken place in the world between 2017 and 2112. The brief summary that Merisi had passed on to Richards in the apartment in Milan when the first time that the two men had met, had provided enough information to convince the young scientist and engineer of the seriousness of Merisi's mission. Now he was to understand the full gravity of the situation.

Given the apocalyptic nature of the world into which he had been transported, Richards was not expecting a Hollywood-style narrative with a happy ending. He was also mindful of the caveat that Argonne had meticulously delivered at the start of the presentation that it had been heavily edited to ensure that he would not be exposed to new sciences and technologies that had not even been dreamt of in the early part of the 21st Century - nevertheless he was shocked, and desperately saddened, to witness some all-to-familiar scenes. They were images of countless multitudes of displaced peoples fleeing conflict and starvation – but on a scale that he had never imagined. There were vast temporary camps for these large swathes of humanity, in the shadow of nameless cities. It was evident that building a large, fortified wall had become the preferred 'solution' to the mass refugee question.

Conspicuously absent were any details of the weapons of future wars, but there were plenty of scenes of armoured, flying, troop carrying vehicles which were the unmistakable hallmarks of warfare. Richards instantly recognised the youthful innocence of the faces that stared out from these troop transporters. In that respect it appeared that human conflict had remained unchanged over many centuries. "So, robots and drones did not manage to supersede humans in the theatre of war, after all," he mused.

If the narrative of human suffering was a familiar one, what surprised Richards was that the vehicles and the weapons, and the other machinery of warfare, appeared not to have the national marks of identity with which he was familiar. There was no sign of the 'stars & stripes,' nor was there any obvious sign of a crescent or a star that might indicate allegiance to a particular religious or political ideology. Instead, the competing 'sides' seemed to identify with different corporate loyalties. Richards was not surprised to observe the GIATCOM logo displayed on vehicles and on vast, warehouse-like establishments. There were also instances where identifying logos were absent, or where a logo or symbol had clearly been 'air brushed out.' When Richards questioned such omissions, Argonne merely responded with an impenetrable "I am not at liberty to divulge that fact" – and Richards had of course, already learnt that it was pointless to try to probe beyond the android's carefully prepared defences.

Generally, the two beings sat in silence as the three-dimensional presentation rolled methodically on. Richards was both enthralled and appalled by what he was seeing. Argonne simply had nothing she was required to add.

The main theme of the narrative was of the destruction of what had once been accepted as 'civilisation.' Frustratingly for Richards, there were few indications of what the so-called 'super cities' had looked like prior to the nuclear conflicts that had led to their destruction – but the scenes of mass devastation were unmistakable, as were the inevitable consequences of the sudden displacement of whole populations of people.

The only crumb of comfort that Richards could see in the

presentation was that the world's 'Uninhabitable Zones,' instead of being vast landscapes of desolation and emptiness, where nothing could grow, appeared to have been 'reclaimed' by nature, and had returned to being undisturbed regions of jungle- like vegetation. That heartened Richards, but the main message came across loud and clear – nuclear conflict had consigned large portions of the world's surface to being unsafe for human habitation. What's more, these areas had formerly been among the most fertile regions of the world, and so it naturally followed that they had been the most heavily populated.

Richards simply had no point of reference for the sheer scale of human suffering that had been instigated by the global conflicts that had taken place. What was made clear from the presentation was that, very close on the heels of the breakdown of civilisation, was the rise of viruses and microbes. Unchecked by the availability of effective antibiotic remedies, diseases spread rapidly among displaced populations. The only effective policy was that of 'abandonment' – "rather a non-policy," thought Richards – and the isolation of vast multitudes of people. What became of the hundreds of thousands of people who were left to fend for themselves in these 'Isolation Zones' was undocumented, and Richards could only speculate as to the horrors brought about by the mass struggle for survival in worlds bereft of order.

What was questionable at this time was how did these pandemic viruses come about? And we still don't know till this day whether definitively the COVID-19 pandemic virus was MANMADE, mainly to improve economic growth to increase the labour market within the global healthcare sector.

There was evidence found from a recruitment advertisement two months prior to the COVID-19 pandemic breakout in October 2019 that an Oxford research company, along with three international academic institutions, looking to expand their research and recruitment drive. In the advertisement, it specified.

'Our client is a new company founded by three academic institutions, the University of Oxford, Imperial College and the London School of Hygiene and Tropical Medicine. It will build a vaccine manufacturing and innovation centre, supporting the development of new vaccines and biological medicines for applications, including gene therapy and cancer therapy. The company will a) provide training, b) develop new methods for manufacturing vaccines at low cost and high productivity, and c) manufacture vaccines for clinical trials and for public deployment, in the event of a disease outbreak in the UK or abroad. The company will be supported by two industrial partners with extensive experience in vaccine manufacturing and development.'

'The company will support the UK economy, for example, by job creation, and by facilitating the commercial development of new vaccines by UK companies. The centre will be used by the UK government to manufacture vaccines rapidly in the event of a pandemic affecting the UK, for example influenza, and it will also enable rapid global response to emerging highly infectious epidemic pathogens such as Ebola and Zika. The centre will innovate new technologies, including manufacture of personalised cancer vaccines and vectors for gene therapy.'

This was published as a recruitment advertisement only two months before COVID-19 outbreak. It was as if they knew the pandemic was going to happen.

It appears they knew at the time; a global pandemic was imminent, like an answer to the trend that was taking place at the time, which was a major increase in the youth of that present day studying research into healthcare related employment. The youth labour market at that time generically had stagnated over the previous two decades, to justify the investment in job creation within the healthcare research sector.

Richards' eye had lit up at the revelation and was quite taken back at how the very conspiracy could well be plausible and realistic as the main driving factor of investment within the health care industry at that time, and how a consortium of organisations could influence and orchestrate such a plan to have a global impact.

The presentation touched upon the history of Richards' own time – or, at least, of the decade immediately following his 'death.' There was a description of how violent crimes increased, year on year, during the early part of the 21st Century, particularly 'hate crimes.' There was also an account of increasing levels of depression within the workplace in Western societies prior to the nuclear conflicts that were to follow.

"There are too many bad people in this world than good, my friend. Wolves in sheep's clothing or should I say androids in human's clothing!"

"Deceit is prevalent even more so in the future. 'The multiplier proxy,' we call it. It became a market and industry in its own right, ever since the dawn of cybercrime in the early part of the 21st century."

"By the mid-21st century, special agents like bounty hunters were hired by government to hunt down private cyber criminals in a multi-billion dollar cyber crime industry. The IT industry made more money off creating anticrime prevention than the IT itself. Crime was feeding the industry's growth. We were creating the bad people for the good of the economy. Which is ethically wrong!"

"No real growth in advancing technology, only cannibalising ourselves."

The presentation described how traumatic experiences led to a variety of mental problems, including Post-traumatic Stress Disorder, and how advances in cognitive behavioural therapy methods, such as Exposure therapy, where patients are exposed to stimuli which provoke fear and anxiety, but in a safe controlled environment, improved treatment for these conditions. It was discovered that brain-derived neurotrophic factor (BDNF) and the N-methyl-D-aspartate receptors (NMDA) were crucial in this process, and that increased acetylation of these two genes led to their transcriptional activation, which increased neural plasticity. This enabled many anxiety disorders to be treated.

Richards recognised the small, yellow tablets that Merisi had given him. He learnt this drug had been developed to induce the exposure therapy process through stimulating both BDNF and NMDA receptors. This part of the presentation was familiar to Richards, as he was well aware of such stimulation being induced by exercise. Very often, when he had experienced a 'mental block', or when he had come across a problem that he was unable to solve, he had found that going out for a run had freed his mind, enabling him to think more clearly. Many of his university colleagues had found the same thing – but he was intrigued to find that a drug had been developed to achieve the same effect. He had also noticed that the pill that Merisi had given him had had a far more powerful and immediate effect than taking exercise.

"Besides stabilising your trauma," Argonne had explained, "and enabling you to give free reign to your ideas, the drug that Merisi gave you has the ability to penetrate the disguise of shapeshifters, by super enhancing the senses. A side effect of the drug you are all too familiar with experiencing before, Doctor."

As they both stared into each other's eyes, Ben realised Argonne knew every little detail of the events of his life that built up to where he was currently now. He couldn't help thinking that his life was planned out for him. He had to go along with UNA's plan to send him back, as it was instrumental to date in help saving his life for the future of others. Besides, there had to be a reason for every incident occurring, like his destiny was set out for him to go back and deliver his ideas by winning the investment and ridding Feng of his intentions.

He could rely on the drug to free him from his trauma of losing his mother and stimulate the generation of his unique ideas for renewable projects. What's more, with his new faster limbs, he had the ability to run for longer and faster to stimulate the BDNF and NMDA receptors long term. This reassured him he was capable of generating ideas more constantly for the long term.

He was now fully equipped to go back and help create a better future.

The presentation continued. Richards was familiar with the concept of 'The Doomsday Clock,' published and updated by the Bulletin of Atomic Scientists, which estimated how close the Earth was to a global disaster, from threats posed by climate change, deteriorating international relations and the proliferation of nuclear weapons. An image shown of this 'clock' indicating that the 'time' was one minute to midnight in 2009, was particularly poignant for Richards.

"And nobody took any notice," he thought to himself.

"Everyone thought it would never happen!"

Statistics were quoted during the presentation, to illustrate how the frequency of wars between countries declined substantially after 1945, but it was emphasised that international warfare had been replaced by violence that was largely domestic in nature, and that overall armed conflict actually increased considerably. What was clear was that in a world where military technology made the total annihilation of civilisation a possibility, there was always a chance that the ultimate calamity might be just around the corner.

The narrative then degenerated to being a story of nuclear conflicts that had been ignited by the struggle for power between nations and conflicting religious ideologies. It was also a story of the irresponsible rejection, on the part of the world's political leaders of a succession of warnings about the dangers of not safeguarding the earth's future through investment in sustainable technologies and renewable energy. This part of the history of course came as no surprise to Dr Ben Richards, who had devoted his life to the promotion of sustainable energy sources. But even he was astounded by the speed of the world's decline, which was initiated by widespread climate-related crop failure in southern parts of Europe, Eastern Europe as far north as The Urals and the western half of the Asian continent. The resulting famines triggered an uncontainable migration of people in all directions from the affected area, but mostly into the more affluent countries of northern Europe.

The social and political tensions caused by such an unprecedented movement of people and clamouring for food and the other necessities for life, inevitably resulted in armed conflict. With the world's superpowers adopting an increasingly entrenched stance on behalf of their traditional allies, it was not long before confrontation became global. To Richards' horror, from the initial launching of inter-continental missiles, it was just a few months before the world's economy lay utterly, and irreversibly in ruins.

Yet, life continued, and if the often predicted destruction of civilization had a familiar ring for Richards, he was surprised by the story of the Earth during the latter half of the 21st Century.

While the large majority of the world's population suffered a chaotic and unimaginable fate, the few to survive unscathed became an isolated but technologically advanced elite. The scientific discoveries of the early part of the century were not forgotten. After most of the traditional global institutions had collapsed and the old political structures had disintegrated, it was the leading hi-tech corporations that filled the power vacuum.

Unhindered by established ethical paradigms, and instead led by the vision of a handful of powerful and visionary entrepreneurs, the frontiers of science and technology advanced in a new direction. The old ideological, political, and religious enmities were forgotten, and with the mortality of the human race itself being thrown sharply into focus, the main agenda for the scientific community became that of the quest for immortality. Such advances had been made in the fields of artificial intelligence, robotics, genetic engineering, and stem cell technology, that renewing the various components of the human body had become commonplace. Life expectancy at least for the economic and social elite, had risen dramatically in the years leading up to the final and devastating nuclear confrontations of the 2060s. All that remained was for those with the financial resources, and a clear view of what might be achieved to put the strands together.

Richards absorbed the presentation with fascination, and no small amount of horror, when it came to the revelations about the world's dramatic decline. But it was the story of how the Enhanced Human Programme had developed, leading to the creation of androids and similar 'life types,' (as the presentation had described them), that intrigued him the most. He now understood a little more of the nature of the likes of Merisi and Shui Feng – and of his own replacement limbs!

"So, how did the rise of Giatcom come about?" asked Richards.

"You see Doctor, before the mid-part of 21st century, China continued to advance in economic growth. Whilst the West appeared to degenerate with their growth largely due to too much emphasis on certain unproductive and saturated markets such as IT software industry. As a result, too many creative industry jobs in AI were created. Capitalism created an adverse effect on Western society, resulting in mental health problems from companies such as Data-con. Without structure and order from markets which followed a collectivism economic model that harnessed a team-oriented work ethic, an individualism economic model promoted too much outsourcing and individualism, causing mistrust, anxiety, mismanaged expectations, and a poor skilled work force. Too much individualism proved to breed narcissism and unproductivity in the West. Creating a society without order or organization, inevitably it evolved into anarchy. Which is why China were on top, and continued to become the most productive country in the world during the early and mid-part of the 21st century, due to their focus more on collectivism rather than individualism as their cultural and economic model. An economy comes to a stand-still if we are all satisfied with rewards from social media and no productive work. Giatcom, being a Chinese company, accelerated their economic growth by investing in pioneering technologies that required large investment in a collectivism way, at the right time during the early part of the 21st century and continued to grow during the mid-part of the 21st century."

"That's worrying for the West!"

"Yes, indeed. You see, Social Learning theorist – BF Skinner researched the effective productivity of getting work produced through carrying out the work first in the form of a cost before reward, which, in effect, is a more socialist economic model."

"The dawn of social media and the expanding work force in creative industries is spawned from capitalism. It is a Reward before Cost economic model. We want more likes and a following, which induces mental health problems, if reward replaces a cost of doing any actual work. If you are rewarded first, you won't do any real work at any real cost. A future society where rewards come first and cost comes second has broken society's order and productivity to progress with infrastructure advancement, spawned by the age of social media rewards being geared towards individualist capitalism and entrepreneurship. Which creates unproductive markets becoming cannibalistic, saturated, and fragmented with capitalism."

"Collectivism has never existed in the West since the 1970s. Narcissism became a ritual habit."

"The West couldn't provide professional or technical workers due to being focused too much on a work force wanting to be too individualist and self-made Directors of our own destiny."

"Our future selves became humanoids to survive as a human race against a multitude of variant viruses, and air pollution due to CO_2 emissions and increasing air temperatures, and humidity due to climate change. A ventilator mask was mandatory to survive as a human."

"We became machine like."

"Reality is masked by illusions," Richards murmured. "This was beyond my imagination."

"Correction Doctor, your own reality is masked by your own illusions."

"It's difficult to know what is reality, and what is an illusion," as he glared at Argonne.

"So, how did the Integration of AI into humans first come about?" enquired Richards.

"Integrating AI into humans was first endorsed by the rich entrepreneurs in the middle of the 21st century, to prolong their life and then used by the government as a form of technological advancement in law in order and defence on an international scale. It later was used in the fight against climate change for human survival, rolled out as a form of advanced vaccine programme to enable to breathe in air polluted environments. AI gradually became a form of eugenics, in the form of 'One had to integrate with AI to survive.' Nonconformists who wished to stay one hundred percent human would eventually die out. To strive to live in the future – eugenics could be adopted to save only the willing to integrate their bodies with AI in order to survive the increasing air pollution and evolve. Humans who refused AI being integrated were part of the eugenics programme – to dispose of, whilst those who agreed to integrate AI into their bodies survived and became part of the eugenics society of humanoids who survived. AI was used with CRISPR technology, which advanced into using AI combined to create biogenetic engineering of humanoids. Allowing the ability to use AI as part of the genome editing to produce an enhanced human being."

"AI was first used with CRISPR on humans to prevent hypoxia from densely air polluted environments, due to climate change and nuclear disasters. It helped genetically engineer improvements in humans' breathing."

"The broken glass can't be fixed, but the people breathing the air inside it, can be fixed. This is how the planet's human habitat survived... by fixing humans' ability to breathe and adapt to increasing air polluted environments due to climate change and nuclear disasters."

"And how do we do that?"

"By having advanced oxygen masks in the future, as part of our bodies."

"But shouldn't we do more by creating prevention in the environment, and the way we use our utilities, transport and live our lives instead?"

"Yes, we are already doing that, but it's too late... too much damage has already been done to the broken glass. We need to continue with rethinking renewable innovations in the environment, but more so, especially with increasing air pollution and airborne mutated viruses already prevalent. We need to rethink how we use the environment in the future and how we can help design it better to survive climate change and avoid manmade disasters. In order to survive!"

"So, it's the redesign of people! Not just the planet that needs to change?"

"Yes!"

"Oh, and the integrated oxygen mask is able to filtrate out toxins in the fluids and solids we consume, besides filtrating the polluted air we breathe."

One other thing that struck Richards was that, although the history that had been recounted to him appeared to be full, frank and factual, and there was a great deal of information on the formation and development of the likes of GIATCOM and the UNA, there had been no mention of the most striking breakthrough – the discovery of how to travel through time. When the presentation had finished, Richards asked Argonne about this.

CHAPTER 2

THE SATOR SQUARE

When the presentation had finished, Richards asked Argonne about the discovery of how to travel through time. "There is no mention of how time travel came about, in your presentation. Why?"

"That is because the capacity for time travel is such a closely guarded secret," she replied. "The UNA will not even speak of it in its own communications. As you can imagine, Dr Richards, in the wrong hands, either now or at some time in the past, such knowledge might have devastating consequences. You will remember that Merisi was very careful not to reveal too many details to you."

Richards scornfully glared at the android, expecting more of an answer.

Richards asks, "Are Caravaggio and Merisi the same person? Is Caravaggio from the past, trained in the future, and sent to protect and assist me?"

"Ah yes, curiosity killed the humanoid."

"No, they are not the same person. Merisi took the name Merisi from the name Michaelangelo Merisi da Caravaggio as his agent name, after meeting Caravaggio on his time travelling adventures. So he is not the same person. Caravaggio stays in the past as the legend. Agent Merisi, who works for UNA, uses Caravaggio's drawings and the concept of his subversive story telling in Caravaggio's drawings to hide messages from the Androids who are unable to understand what these messages are conveying due to AI lacking creative and emotional intelligence. Merisi is trained in the future, modifying Caravaggio's drawings himself to create messages for you, Dr Richards. As the shapeshifting of the Androids could be anywhere listening when Merisi is speaking to you Dr Richards. Merisi is sent from the future to protect and assist you, Ben," explains Argonne.

"But how did time travel come about?" asked Richards frantically.

"Ok, I can tell you this much –

That Time travel portals were initially created in 2110 after seventy years of research and development. They were initially built to enable you to go back in time, from the date it was created. The time travel portals were sent from the future to be opened in holy places one hundred years years BC in the form of a coded relic – The SATOR SQUARE, which is why the church found them and kept it a secret for generations. Until some people of that time had gone missing, travelling in time. I believe the man who founded that mission was a man called Jason Riaz. Riaz, who came from our future in 2110, travelled to this year 2049 to try and stop the recent nuclear disaster in China occurring, and in the process got killed. We think it is likely to do with GIATCOM. The time travel portals are incapable of travelling forward in time past 2118, as this is the date when Armageddon happens due to too much extreme climate change weather, and too many more nuclear disasters. Do you hear Dottore!"

"The portals become demolished due to too many nuclear and climate change disasters occurring up until 2118, when the environment finally says it's had enough. So travelling to the future has a limit of 2118."

"So, what have you learnt from your future, Dr Richards?" Richards paused before answering.

"It is certainly shocking to see the world I once knew – a world that still exists, in my time - crumble so completely, and so violently," he replied, at last. "But it is heartening for me to find that those who have survived the apocalypse appear to be building a better future and striving to create a better human race."

"There has certainly been the birth of a different race," said Argonne. "Although it is difficult for me to make a judgement on what might be better."

"Is that because of your life type?" asked Richards, starting to get to grips with the range of humanoids and androids that now inhabited the world.

"It's because I have no concept of 'humanity' in the way that you would understand it. I am designed so that I can show emotion, in response to certain stimuli – but I have no way of making a valid appraisal of whether a given attribute of humanity, or a given course of actions, is 'good' or 'bad.' Good for what, or for whom?"

Richards did not answer Argonne's question. For one thing, it appeared to be rhetorical – but also, he was reluctant to enter into a philosophical discussion about humanity with an android!

"But what you have witnessed," continued Argonne, "is that some members of the human race have in the past few decades learnt by humanity's mistakes, and it is only natural that they have sought to take a different direction. In the years leading up to the destruction of the previous, long-established civilisation, the human race, as a whole, became increasingly more violent. Most of those who survived the catastrophe took on a more phlegmatic personality, being much less inclined to be driven by emotion. However, because we are now in an age where individualism is stronger than patriotism, some sectors of society have lost touch with the emotional side of humanity. These are the ones who have led the drive for personal success and wealth."

Argonne was equipped with enough emotional sensibility to realise that Richards was troubled by what he had seen.

"I understand that this is all a lot to take in, Dr Richards," she said. "Would you like to have a break before we move on to the next stage of your briefing?"

"'The next stage?" exclaimed Richards. "You mean that there is more information to take in?"

"Yes, of course. There is very important work that we want you to do for us – much that needs to be put right – so we have to make sure that you are fully briefed and fully prepared, before we send you back. You need to be physically and mentally prepared." There was something in the term 'mentally prepared' that Richards found to be slightly ominous.

"'Mentally prepared?" he asked, raising an eyebrow. "Yes. We have identified certain frailties in your psychological make- up – certain things that might prevent you from fulfilling your full potential in the way that we would like."

"So, you think you know me?" asked Richards, rather sceptically, given that he had always been confident that he was the expert on the subject of his own mind and thoughts.

"We know you extremely well, Dr Richards. In fact, you have become one of the most studied and analysed individuals in history. We have had teams of experts analysing every event in your life, and we have built up a very detailed psychological profile."

Richards now looked at Argonne with both eyebrows raised, with an expression that betrayed both surprise and a little indignation.

"Of course, we can go through this tomorrow," continued Argonne. "Time is one thing that we have on our side."

"No, I am very keen to address these 'psychological' issues straight away. So, in what way are you suggesting that I am lacking psychologically?"

Again, Argonne was fully capable of detecting a hint of scepticism and even reluctance in Ben's tone of voice.

"Well, a major issue identified has been your relationships with women throughout your life. Your feelings for your mother, in particular."

The sudden reference to his mother surprised Richards. "And what do you know about my mother?" he snapped.

"What have you people been doing? Have you had probes inside my head, or something?"

Argonne smiled. It was a trained smile. A smile designed to reassure a patient.

"We have gathered a great deal of information on the impact

of your mother's unfortunate death, and the circumstances surrounding it. We know you were traumatised, and that you initially had treatment for a high anxiety disorder." This was a surprise for Richards, as he had little recollection of the immediate aftermath of his mother's death – but he said nothing. "After a while, it was a family friend – a priest – who took care of you and attended to your emotional needs."

"Yes. Father Luigi."

"And we actually sent an investigator back to 1994, to speak to Father Luigi, to learn more about how the young Ben Richards was affected by the incident."

"You did what?"

"It was a calculated risk, of course. As you know, we use the facility to travel through time very sparingly, because of the risks involved, but we consider this period in your life to have been very important. Character-defining, in fact."

Richards was still coming to terms with the revelation that UNA had sent someone to effectively interview Father Luigi — about his emotional state.

"So, when I was a little boy..." he began.

"Please don't think that we sent a robot to kidnap your friend and guardian, and interrogate him," interrupted Argonne. "The priest met a pleasant middle-aged lady, who had two or three polite conversations with him. It was all very discrete and made a negligible impact on events. We are very professional and very proficient, you know."

"So, what do you think you know about the incident with my mother?" asked Richards.

"Well, we know you cried out to her time and time again, but to no avail. You told Father Luigi that many times. You also told him about the recurring nightmares you had, for several weeks after your mother's death. You told him many times, about how you screamed so loud that your throat became quite sore – but no sound came from your mouth. Sometimes you woke up suddenly, screaming your mother's name. Do you remember those dreams, doctor?"

Richards nodded. "Yes, I remember them very well," he confessed. "Mainly because I have had them, on and off, ever since that day."

"Well, appraising these dreams in the context of subsequent events in your life, and your subsequent behaviour, the conclusion of our analysts is that the fundamental psychological trauma that you suffered was in not being able to make your voice heard. Your voice was apparently not strong enough to save your mother, and since then you have felt that your voice has not been heard by others."

"Analysing the tone and the language you have used in numerous speeches and presentations at conferences and seminars, the respected speaker on the stage is still the little boy on the shoreline, calling out to his mother. Your determination to make your voice heard is what has driven you as an individual, to pursue your ideas and make sure that someone hears them. But you have also had issues with self-perception. You are too self-critical, and fundamentally you lack self-belief. Of course, this is very different from the way in which others perceive you and your ideas. You must have confidence that other people believe in your ideas, and they want to help you achieve your aims. You do not have to be vocal to be a great leader. Your vocation is to be a thought leader, and you do not need to continue with an endless circuit of conferences and seminars in order to convince people."

"Human beings don't just see the world; they actively interpret what they see. Depending on what they are expecting to see. How many times have you seen or heard things the wrong way?"

Argonne did not wait for an answer.

"Let me show you an example of when you didn't see what you thought you saw," she continued, and without making a perceptible movement or gesture to create the illusion, both she and Ben Richards were instantly immersed in a three-dimensional image of the tightrope artist performing a walk near the Ponte Vecchio, in Florence – except that the action was unfolding in slow motion.

"What is this?" asked Richards, in wonder.

"You know what it is, Dr Richards. You were there."

"But, how? How did you get this image?"

"Merisi was there – as you now know. He will have made an

ongoing surveillance record for later analysis and reconstruction. Now, watch!"

Having briefly paused the action with a wave of her hand, Argonne set the scene in motion once again, but this time at a slower speed than before. Richards looked around him in all directions. He could see the tightrope walker in front of him, and the crowd below, anxiously looking up. Then he turned around, and to his amazement he could see himself on the balcony.

"Watch what happens here, Doctor," exclaimed Argonne, gesturing towards the man on the tightrope.

Richards looked over his left shoulder to see the performer shooting a dart from a tiny implement that was attached to his left wrist, just as he fell from the tightrope. As the dart travelled slowly past Richards, he recognised it as the strange object that he picked up from the floor of the balcony just seconds later. He also had the distinct impression that the walker had deliberately allowed himself to fall from the tightrope into the water. "Probably to distract the crowd's attention from where the dart was going," he thought to himself.

Following the trajectory of the dart, Richards saw how Merisi with his eyes fixed firmly on the projectile had moved the camera to intercept it. Richards turned to Argonne to ask her how on earth Merisi was able to track the dart, at the speed that it was travelling – before aborting the question. He was mindful of the superhuman qualities that his friend possessed.

"You see, Doctor," explained Argonne, "you had only heard a loud 'crack,' and then saw that your camera had been broken. You were unaware that something had been fired at you, and that Merisi had intervened to protect you. That's because, as individuals we perceive events in different ways, and so we interpret them differently. We all have a unique point of view and perspective. It was the same situation with your mother, when she was in the sea. From your point of view, it was obvious that you were screaming at your mother, warning her of the approaching tsunami – but your mother could see nothing more than a child jumping up and down and waving."

Richards understood what Argonne was trying to tell him that there was nothing more that he could have done to save his mother's life. For the first time, after all the anxiety that the incident had caused him, over many years, he was beginning to feel more at peace with himself. From the 'big picture' of saving civilisation as he knew it, his thoughts were now very much focused on the image of the small boy on the beach who was calling out to his mother. It remained a bitter memory, and he felt some pangs of guilt that he had been saved by Merisi in Florence, when his mother could not be saved, however hard he yelled.

But then he resolved to move forward and confront the task that had been put in front of him. He reflected on everything else that Argonne had said to him and understood that she was helping him to become a better person. It was clear that she knew of the many traumas from his past, and that it was important for him to put them behind him. Richards resolved to follow the guidance that the UNA had clearly and meticulously put together for him. He decided that he would do everything he could to live up to the high expectations that the world had of him.

"I think I understand what you are telling me, and I will not let you down," he declared to Argonne. "What is it you need me to do?"

Argonne held up a hand, a gesture designed to calm Richards' impatience.

"There is much for you to do, back in your own time, but there is still much that I need to teach you. You also need much more training in the use of your new arm, if you are to use it to its full potential."

"So how much longer do you think I need before I am ready?"

"Patience, Doctor. We need to be absolutely sure that you have everything you need for your assignment. For instance, how is your Japanese?"

"Japanese? Why Japanese?"

"Because your first assignment will be to attend the World Climate Change -Kyoto Summit in Tokyo. That is also Merisi's target. His mission is to ensure that the world leaders who will be gathered there make the correct decisions, in terms of investment in sustainable energy sources – and the world needs Dr Ben Richards to be the spearhead and the inspiration for that drive."

"Merisi will be posing as a young, but very influential economist called Professor Richard Bryce-Fairbrother. Do you know him?"

"Yes. I met him once – briefly. I didn't like him very much."

"Well, you will be pleased with the knowledge that in Kyoto, if all goes according to plan, Bryce-Fairbrother will actually be your friend, as Merisi."

Richards was heartened by that thought, and relished the opportunity to work alongside Merisi.

"It would also be a great surprise," added Argonne, "if Shui Feng were not also planning to attend the Summit – so you will have to be at your best, both mentally and physically. For both your sake and Merisi's sake, and for the sake of us all."

The prospect of encountering Feng was not something that Richards looked forward to, yet he was determined to not be deterred.

"So – what's next, then?" he asked.

"For a start, there is much information that we need to upload to your brain," replied Argonne. Richards was slightly disturbed by that particular expression, but he had become accustomed to not understanding every nuance of what the android said to him, so he didn't interrupt.

"You may also want to revisit the familiar places of your youth," continued Argonne, "to help you find where your true journey of leadership began and understand that unfulfilled futures are merely branches of the past – dead branches. This journey to the future will help you discover the truth about yourself and enable you to recover your past. Look for the positive mirror image that recognises the truth in you and your surroundings. Discover much more that is yours and what you can give, by realising what you have been gifted with, and which you will always have."

"And how might I do that?"

"That is our next task. Follow me..."

CHAPTER 3

FUTURE REALITY OF ARTIFICAL INTELLIGENCE

Argonne left the room at a brisk walk. Richards followed, occasionally breaking into a jog for a few paces, in order to keep up. The sterile air-conditioned corridors of the UNA establishment were deserted, but anyone observing the pair might have been amused at Richards' rather child-like efforts to keep pace with Argonne. In truth he had felt rather like a child in a sweet shop since his arrival in 2112, trying to absorb every facet of what he was experiencing. This was in spite of the fact that Argonne had been following a very strict protocol in terms of what Richards was allowed to see and know. He could not help bombarding the very amenable android with questions, such was his curiosity as a scientist. Up to a certain point, these questions were answered fully and patiently – but when he approached the boundary of what the UNA was prepared for him to know, Argonne responded with an emotionless, "I cannot tell you that." And Richards learnt very quickly that it was pointless to try to trick her into exceeding her prescribed limits. Although this was a being, or a machine that had a limited emotional range, it was obvious to him that she was equipped with a high level of intelligence.

What appeared to be a very clear constraint imposed upon him was that he was not permitted to interact with, or even see any of the citizens of the 22nd Century world to which he had been transported – and his sole companion at this time had confirmed that this was by design. Frustratingly, Argonne was 'not authorised' to explain the reasons for this policy. It came as a major surprise to Richards, when he and Argonne approached a pair of large slate grey double doors, which opened up to reveal a large room full of people.

Argonne stopped a few yards inside this room and glanced across at Richards. She was able to accurately read the startled expression on his face.

"People!" he exclaimed, unable for the moment to properly construct a question to alleviate his confusion. But it was not necessary, as Argonne had already started to explain.

"I thought you might be surprised," she said. "But there is no issue with you entering this space, as you will not be able to interact with these people. They are all strictly incommunicado." Richards gazed around the vast room, and soon noticed that the majority of people were seated at what appeared to be some sort of workstation, consisting of a reclined and generously padded chair, and a shallow dome above each person's head which appeared to be projecting a 360-degree image around them. Richards could see that the people nearest to him were wearing an opaque visor over their eyes and large headphones. Some were gesticulating with their arms and muttering words he could not understand above the general soft murmur of voices and the pumped-out 'muzak' that appeared to serve no purpose. Each person had his or her own separate space within a square grid pattern. Estimating the number of rows and columns in front of him, Richards quickly calculated that there must have been more than two thousand people in the room. As far as he could tell, whoever these people were they represented a range of age groups – although there was a marked majority of men in the room, and there were no children.

In among the rows of reclined seats, at roughly regular intervals, there were standing figures observing the activity in the room. Richards guessed that these were androids. He was unsure whether the scene reminded him more of a typing pool or a concentration camp.

"So – what is this place?" Richards asked, at length. "What are all these people doing?"

"They are working – in a sense," replied Argonne, in a slightly cryptic tone of voice that both surprised and impressed Richards. He turned his head to observe the android closely. "So, what are they doing – exactly?" he asked.

"This one here," said Argonne, pointing to the man who was seated nearest to her, "is a civil engineer, and he is currently working on a major bridge building project. The man next to him is a schoolteacher, and he..." Argonne hesitated for a moment, as if waiting for some information to reach her, "...is working on creating new material for the coming academic year. The man next to him is a nano technologist, who..."

"Okay. I get the idea," interrupted Richards, raising a hand in order to stop Argonne from describing the 'activity' of every being in the room. "So, this chap here is doing some civil engineering?"

"Yes."

"Just using his mind to create the plans, I suppose?"

"Yes. Or at least in his virtual world. Obviously, he is not working on an actual project. It would be absurd for a human to be engaged in the real activity when it is possible for an android to draw up plans for achieving the same result, and with a choice of many alternative designs a thousand times faster."

"So, all of these people are working on projects and tasks that are not actually real?"

"It is real for them, Dr Richards. It is their reality. It is many decades since humans last worked on such tasks. Great advances in the development of what was called 'Future Reality of Artificial Intelligence,' made many highly educated and highly trained people redundant in their own field. Either they accepted fairly menial work that consisted of following precise instructions issued to them by an android, or they descended into worklessness. Unlike the masses, whose manual jobs were replaced by robots and other machines, the more highly qualified members of society found the very rapid transition towards a state of redundancy very hard to accept, and this caused an epidemic of mental health issues. All of the people in this room will have been referred here as a result of a diagnosis of a mental health issue related to depression, most of them suffering with a crisis of self-worth and self-esteem."

"So, this is part of a process of rehabilitation? I assume they are sent back into mainstream society once they have been cured of their mental health issues?"

"Very occasionally – but why would anyone wish to do that? They have everything they need here. Some have been here for many years and have formed relationships and had children."

"But only in a virtual world. Nothing of what they experience in this room is real," protested Richards.

"No, but they experience it, as you have just said – just as you experience your version of reality. You have answered your own query."

Richards suddenly felt utterly at a loss to form an argument against the android's watertight logic – a feeling that had become all too familiar during his period of 'training' with her.

"Shall we move on?" asked Argonne, who then waited patiently for Richards to agree to follow her to the next destination in his carefully planned itinerary – a schedule that had no doubt been planned by an android just like Argonne, or by a similarly advanced piece of machinery.

Richards glanced around the room just once more, observing the apparently largely lifeless sample of humanity that was neatly arrayed in the vast space. And he had one more question for Argonne: "I don't suppose you have anybody in this room who specialises in the generation of sustainable energy using wind turbines..." he asked.

Argonne's programming picked up the rhetorical tone of Richards' question from a combination of his facial expression and the tone of his voice.

"Quiet," she said, and her face immediately contorted into a pleasant smile that Richards had come to understand, it meant "that's the end of the conversation." Argonne knew Richards knew this – and so she immediately turned and began to walk briskly in the direction of a large double door.

Again, Richards followed her, as she left the large space and entered a long straight gallery. To the left of this gallery, separated by a large and continuous pane of glass, there was a rectangular space that was much smaller than the one they had just left – and this time there was far more animation among the people that Richards could see there. All were dressed in the same 'uniform' as those who were ensconced in their virtual world, but this time the people appeared to be separated into individual sections in front of screens that appeared to Richards to be much more like orthodox workstations.

Argonne suddenly stopped walking, as she sensed her trainee had paused to observe the scene through the glass. He noticed that all the people wearing the uniform were engaged in an activity of some sort, and almost all of them were showing some outward signs of anxiety. He watched one man, with a receding hair-line – who looked like he might be in his mid- forties – as he sat in front of a large blue screen, mopping his dank brow with his sleeve. Suddenly, the man rose from his seat, walked in a small 360-degree circle around his plastic seat, and then sat down again. He then continued to look agitated as he resumed whatever task had been set for him. A little to his left another man, probably about fifteen years his junior, sat with his left foot tapping rapidly whilst scratching his left arm to quell some imaginary itch. He was also swinging from side to side in what looked like a black leather and chrome swivel chair. Another man entered the door of his allotted space, touched the back of his seat as if he was about to sit down, but then turned and left through the door again. Towards the back of this room, which Richards estimated to contain about twenty people, all of whom displayed some outward sign of anxiety, a grown man wept pathetically. As with all the others seated at a workstation, he was being observed with a careful detachment that could only have been provided by an artificial being of some sort. It was not difficult for Richards to work out what was happening here.

"I suppose these are new arrivals?" he asked Argonne, who was now standing next to him. "Being assessed?"

"Yes. This is the initial screening stage. They have not yet been fully immersed in a virtual world – but they will have been set hypothetical tasks, so that their needs can be assessed."

Richards spent several seconds watching what was going on and could not help feeling sympathy for his fellow human beings. He wondered just how much of the anxiety that was clear from the people's body language was actually due to being set tasks in a laboratory environment by a seemingly unsympathetic android – but decided that he did not want to debate the issue with Argonne. However, he did begin to wonder about the extent to which he too, might be about to be treated like a 'lab rat.' He felt it might be worth asking the question....

"Well, this is all very intense," he said to the android, who was waiting patiently, and in silence by his side. "Do you have something similar planned for me in the next stage of my training?"

"No. None of your mental disorders can be addressed in this way," replied Argonne. Not for the first time, Richards was slightly disconcerted by the android's blunt frankness, and wondered what disorders this technologically advanced world had diagnosed for him – but Argonne continued speaking, not allowing Richards to query her statement: "What we need to do now is to equip you with the knowledge you will need in order to complete the mission that you are being trained for."

"Ah. This is where you download the knowledge into my brain?" he asked. "So, what will you do? Will you deliver some artificial intelligence into my head? Like a computer download? Wirelessly, I hope."

Argonne detected a note of apprehension in the young man's voice.

"All we need to do is to provide you with the necessary links to the pool of knowledge that all androids use. You might be able to understand this by thinking of it as being like 'the Cloud' that you have in your time. It is not something that we do for many humans – mainly because few would be able to use such an information source effectively – but we think you might benefit from it, with the necessary mental training and conditioning. And we no longer recognise the term 'artificial intelligence.'

Intelligence is just intelligence – just as knowledge is knowledge and a reality is a reality."

Richards did not bother to try to get his head around the possible implications of what Argonne had said during that final sentence. He had more pressing practical concerns.

"So, you won't be inserting computer chips or transistors into my head then?" he asked, hopeful that there was no chance that Argonne might have anything like this in mind.

"You will need a receiver of some kind, of course," replied Argonne. "It is possible to attach it to the inside of your skull – but it will also work perfectly well in your pocket."

CHAPTER 4

FORM IS TEMPORARY, CLASS IS PERMANENT

Merisi switched off his communicator. The portal was now closed. Even he with his vast experience in the field, suddenly felt very alone in that dark and silent ancient basement. Merisi was no stranger to working alone, but he was feeling a strange sense of detachment from the young man that he had just sent on the adventure of his short life, and who was instantly some five thousand miles, and almost a hundred years away.

"Maybe it is because of my complete vulnerability, given the forces that are operating around me," Merisi thought to himself, but consoled by his total confidence that both Richards and Grazia Rossini would be well looked after by his colleagues at the UNA, he refocused his attention on his next extremely important task.

But first he had to leave the ruins of Pompeii without being detected by GIATCOM's operatives. The thought of his long-time nemesis Shui Feng, being close by was enough to banish from his mind any musings he had about Ben Richards' reactions to life in the 22nd Century. Very quietly and carefully Merisi climbed the flight of stone steps, and immediately was refreshed by the cool night air.

He paused at the top of the steps, and looked around the ancient ruin, listening intently. It was still an hour before dawn, and all was still. He slipped away, back in the direction that he had come with Ben Richards, cautiously moving from column to column. He was approaching the lifeless body of one of the two GIATCOM androids that he had terminated earlier, when suddenly, the silence was broken by the muffled sound of a woman's voice. It was a single syllable of protest – not a cry for help, but certainly one of pain or discomfort.

Merisi stopped and listened even more intently. He scanned the scene around what was once a luxurious atrium that was once full of colourful works of art, exotic plants and the laughter and scuttling footsteps of children. Now, all was sterile and lifeless, so any noise at ll was magnified, and echoed around the bare stone. Merisi knew he was not alone in the ruin, but the unmistakable tone and pitch of a young woman's voice was something that he did not expect – and it troubled him greatly.

He softly made his way in the direction from which he thought the sound had come. Then there was the sound of footsteps. They came from the entrance to the larger cellar of the town house. Merisi immediately hid himself behind a column. He detected three pairs of feet on the steps. Two betrayed an even, confident gait, but the third pair mounted the steps at an irregular pace that suggested that they were being forced.

"Figlio di puttana!"

The curse pierced the night air, loud and clear. But, more than that, Merisi recognised the voice as belonging to Grazia Rossini! All at once, the reality of the situation dawned on Merisi. It was with some horror that he realised that the person who he had gladly sent to accompany Ben Richards to the UNA's top secret secure establishment in Beijing, the Agency's last remaining stronghold, could be none other than Shui Feng.

A little more than a minute earlier, Merisi had felt a sense of relief and quiet elation. A sense of having accomplished the first important part of his mission. Now he was desperately trying to come to terms with the reality that his complacency and lack of caution might have put the entire operation, and much, much more besides, in jeopardy. How could he have been deceived so easily by Shui Feng? He realised that, as a master of disguise and impersonation himself, he should have been alert to the possibility that Feng could have appeared in the guise of just about anybody. Now of course, it all seemed a very obvious use. Grazia had been in Feng's custody for a long time – and the young damsel tied to a stone plinth was always going to provide compelling bait.

Merisi stood for several seconds, pressing the back of his head hard against the unyielding column, his eyes tightly shut. His prime concern was for the extreme danger that Ben Richards was now in as a result of such an error, but Merisi also feared for the fate of the ancient drawings, whose recovery had been a crucial element of his mission. He was also well aware of the number of very senior members of the UNA who might have been compromised.

"Oh my God," he thought. "There is very definitely a fox in the chicken coop!" It was an expression that he had heard Caravaggio himself use many times – usually mostly in jest, when telling Merisi of one of his close shave escapades. But the metaphor was now a pretty accurate description of a dire situation.

A second, heartfelt curse from Grazia Rossini jolted Merisi from his mental self-flagellation. The young woman and her captors were now close by. Merisi realised that Ben Richards was not the only person he should be protecting who was now in grave danger.

Grazia had a fear of being trapped in the form of Cleithrophobia. She began to have flashbacks of being trapped as a little girl amongst the rumble of a building that collapsed due to an earthquake.

She became overcome with fear and struggled to set herself free. She suddenly remembered her leadership skills as a child from being the best athlete for her age where she lived.

She cast her mind back to when she was hyperventilating and feeling completely empty with nothing left, after finding a second wind of positivity under gruelling circumstances, which she held as an unbelievable and magical moment. Only a few people will experience this in their lifetime. She was blessed that day and it meant more than the world to her to have lived this experience. She needed to draw upon that experience right now and emulate her natural inner strength of bravery and leadership.

Her time that day was the fifth fastest time overall out of approximately 55,500 kids from approximately 250 kids per race over 222 races held over the six weeks summer holidays, over thirty-seven years, was some achievement.

"The day I gave everything," she muttered to herself, "And today I need to give more!"

She recalled the vivid detail of how the race unfolded that day.

* * * * *

She ran flat out in the first mile of a five-kilometre race, to find herself about 200 or 300 metres ahead of everyone else, and then her cardio blew up. As she ran the second mile along the beach front - wind blowing whilst running in sand, she had reached her lactate threshold, resulting in her breathing being restrained and within a minute she found herself going from first to second, to third to fourth (which were all incidentally spread out about fifty metres behind each other). Suddenly she found herself about 300 metres behind first place (who incidentally was her friend at the time, but because she had a mouth on her, she would never live it down if her friend were to beat her in the race). Her friend had trained all year to beat her in that race. She had an off year regarding running performance due to puberty at thirteen. But as the old saying goes; **Form is temporary, Class is permanent.** Probably her most defining race ever, which typified natural bravery and leadership by pushing herself to the absolute limit and running into the unknown. Something inside her head said, "You are not going to let this big head make your life hell by beating you. She can't beat you at something you are much better at naturally! She can't take that away from you."

She thought at that given second, whilst hyper-ventilating, she would rather die in this race than be beaten. Seriously, that was how much that race meant to her. Forget about A star!! Winning races was all that mattered to her.

So she went past third place, who said "What are you doing?"

She said, "I am going to catch her and win!"

"How is that possible, your miles behind!" third place said.

"Watch!" And she just took off again and got into second place as she came off the beach and entered the castle's grounds. She caught up to her friend in first place with a mile to go, and just flew straight passed her into first place as if she was running a mile race. The now second place runner shouted, "What are you doing, are you mad, you mad woman, we have another mile to go and there's a big hill?" (As her friend had ran the race before and she hadn't). In the end she beat her by almost two minutes, about 600 metres and that too on a hill finish. She collapsed lying on the ground afterwards, fighting the dizziness of stopping herself from passing out, but with an ambiguous grimace that broke out into a smile as she tried to comprehend at what she had just done. Like being in a trance from total surprise at what she had achieved, she dropped her head in complete exhaustion. She couldn't have given anymore. She looked at her result and it was the fifth fastest school girl ever to have run the inaugural mini - marathon – five-kilometre race on the Island of Capri since the camp holidays were introduced since 1951. That was the summer of 1988 when she raced. So, it would have been approximately thirty-seven years of six weeks holiday equating to 222 races over them thirty-seven years, and it had kids attending from all over Italy going to that camp. When she looked back, that was by far the gutsiest performance she had ever raced. Definition of running on complete emptiness physically and mentally. To have a massive lead, then physically drained of energy, mentally tortured by going down into fourth and to then comeback from the dead physically and mentally, to then have a **double kick** as a second lease of life, and to be able to run the last thirty-perecnt of the race like a sprint again. With the audacity and bravery of not knowing the end in sight, never mind not knowing that there was a long hill to run at the end, after already hitting lactate badly. She had ran giving absolutely everything! It was a testament of pure spiritual will power. Demonstrating a remarkable double kick, by having a second wind within the turbulent wind, whilst running in sand.

* * * * *

At once she had calmed her presence of mind, in the knowledge that she was a true natural leader, and just had to stay calm and level-headed to be able to get out of her predicament.

Merisi listened as the three sets of footsteps passed by on the other side of the column. As soon as he was satisfied that they had passed the column, he could approach them unseen from behind. Merisi silently slipped out from the shadow. His pure white garb now shone brightly in the moon's light, which now looked down from directly above the ancient ruin – but such was the speed of Merisi's attack that detection was not going to foil him in his objective.

First, he felled the android nearest to him with a crude bludgeoning blow to the back of the head. Then, as Grazia with a startled shriek instinctively ducked her head, Merisi seized the other android around the neck with his left arm, instantly forcing him to the ground. It then took just a split second for the UNA's oldest and most trusted asset to partially decapitate his prey. In spite of the ferocity and intensity of the attack, it was bloodless, due to the physiology of the androids. Apart from the noise of a metallic 'scrunch,' was heard, as the communication circuits between the android's head and body were severed. Merisi had also disposed of his enemy in silence. Nevertheless, when Merisi turned, he saw Grazia Rossini down on one knee, cowering with fear.

"Don't worry, my dear," he assured her. "You are quite safe now."

"Oh, I'm so glad that it's you!" cried Grazia, and spontaneously rested her forehead on Merisi's shoulder, and broke into a fit of relieved sobbing.

It was some time before Grazia had recovered enough

composure to be able to speak, but during this time Merisi removed the bonds which tied her wrists and led her gently to the stone plinth where ironically Shui Feng had posed as her. Merisi said nothing, as the plinth was a reminder of the grave error that he had committed, and he was deep in thought, pondering the possible consequences of what he had done. This thought was soon followed by him touching the right side of his temple as if to switch an invisible button to engage good thoughts in his frontal lobe. He replayed his actions with the androids he had terminated a moment earlier, and felt content he had made up his earlier mistake by saving Grazia. The words, **Form is temporary, Class is permanent** – appeared on his computer screened hologram image that projected in front of his eyes. Only he could see this image. It was a reinforcement mechanism programmed by UNA to engage their humanoids with optimism whilst on duty or in the field of battle. Recalling their good actions, to supersede their bad actions of poor form or experience of bad circumstances. He was reassured that he had class.

"And Ben? Where is Ben? Is he here?" asked Grazia once her convulsive sobbing had subsided.

Merisi looked at her gravely – and his expression struck fear into her heart.

"Ben! What has happened to him?" she demanded.

"I do not know. I am not certain," Merisi replied, with a doleful shake of the head.

Merisi described everything that had happened that night, but he was unable to provide Grazia with any reassurance about the fate of Ben Richards. Grazia too, began to fear the worst – as she had witnessed Shui Feng's cold and calculating nature at close quarters. She had been able to detect not a hint of sympathy or humanity in him during her time in captivity. She placed a consoling hand on Merisi's shoulder.

"What's the old saying- We're all human...and we all make mistakes. There is nothing we can do to help Ben right now," continued Merisi. "As soon as I get news of him, I will let you know. But I need to focus on what I have to do in the present, for there is a great deal to do. My objective now is the Kyoto Summit, which is due to take place in Tokyo in about three weeks time. Do you know about this?"

"Yes, of course," replied Grazia. "It's a big climate change conference to discuss the Kyoto Protocol."

"Well, I need to have a seat at that table. It's vitally important that I am able to steer the discussion in the right direction."

Grazia stared at Merisi, open-mouthed. In spite of all the seemingly impossible things that she had witnessed over the past few days – shape shifting androids included – this idea appeared to her to be the most far-fetched.

"But – this is an international summit. All the heads of the major governments in the world will be there. It's not something that you can just walk into – not even you! Besides, there will be layers upon layers of security, and..."

"Yes, I am aware of that," said Merisi, "but I have a plan." Grazia raised her eyebrows, her expression indicating that she was 'all ears.' "What I need to do," continued Merisi, "is to infiltrate the main meeting of the summit. It's not all that difficult for me to do, but I will probably need some help. How would you like to come with me on a trip to Tokyo?"

"To the summit, you mean?"

"Yes."

"And – how do you think I will be able to get into an event like that?"

"You're a journalist, aren't you?"

"Well, yes. But..."

"All you need is clearance. You just need the appropriate security tag around your neck – and I'm sure that your editor would be delighted with you if you had an invitation to this event?" Grazia didn't answer, but it was obvious that an invitation to Tokyo would be a major coup, both for the young, aspiring journalist, and for the environmentalist magazine that she had joined, straight from university, just eighteen months previously. "I thought so," continued Merisi. "Well, organising the invitation for you is probably the least difficult part of my plan. But first," he said, glancing around at the lifeless carcasses of GIATCOM androids, that formed a shapeless black mound, in the gloom of the ruined Roman town house, "I need to dispose of our friends here."

"Why not just let them rot?" suggested Grazia, unable to hide her contempt and hatred for her former captors.

"No, I'm afraid these things won't rot, as you put it," replied Merisi, "and I don't think it will do very much for this place as a tourist attraction! But the main issue is that I cannot leave this 22nd Century technology for people to find. Can you imagine the consequences if the people of today were to reverse engineer these things?"

Grazia shuddered. Her memories of witnessing the ruthless way in which Shui Feng and his androids had murdered the attraction's night security staff were still very raw.

"So, what are you going to do, then?" she asked. "Do you expect me to help you to bury them?"

"'Bury them? No. Nothing like that," replied Merisi. "If you promise not to breathe a word to a living soul, I will demonstrate the 22nd century art of waste disposal. It will only take about ten to fifteen minutes. Watch..."

CHAPTER 5

DEVIL IN THE DETAIL

The door of Room 1001 of the Cerulean Tower Hotel in Tokyo opened. Soon after, the corpulent figure of Tony Clark, entrepreneur, racehorse owner and Chairman of Norwich City Football Club, entered, and wearily threw a large, claret, leather suitcase onto the nearest of two twin beds. The dark grey Aquascutum trench coat glistened with raindrops from the sharp November shower that had greeted Clark as he dashed from the taxi to the opulent entrance of the 5-star hotel.

Habitually, he reached for the remote-control device on the room's leather covered desk and switched on the TV. As in all of the hotel's rooms, the television was initially pre-set to the CNN News channel – and there was a single news story which was dominating the airwaves: the 2017 United Nations Climate Change Conference, which was due to take place in the city during the ensuing fortnight.

The panel discussion of the conference that was in progress in the CNN studio, reminded Clark of the precious and hard won ID badge he carried in his inside jacket pocket. It was a badge of distinction, as much as an item of security-related paraphernalia, and one which gave him the highest level of security clearance, and virtually free access to the Heads of Delegation of the major industrial powers of the world. Carefully – lovingly, almost – he hung the badge, which dangled from its purple ribbon on the clothes hanger that carried the suit that he was planning to wear for the first day of the conference in two days time.

Tomorrow – a Sunday – was to be used for 'networking.' That meant showing his face to and ingratiating himself with as many influential conference attendees as he could find. Most of whom were staying in that very hotel – and most of whom had a similar idea.

Because of his social and educational background, Tony Clark was a natural 'outsider,' not having gone to school with a member of Her Majesty's Cabinet. However, his success as a businessman and his open moral and financial support for the quest for cleaner, sustainable and economically viable sources of energy, had established him as one of the UK's leading Captains of Industry. His prominence in his home region of East Anglia had earned him the accolade of an honorary PhD, from one of Cambridge University's leading colleges, – a privilege that he had accepted rather sheepishly, in June of the previous year. Admitting that his knowledge of the sciences that were studied and developed by the College's scholars amounted to little more than the contents of Norwich City's trophy cabinet. Nevertheless, he had become a familiar face and voice on local television and radio.

There was of course a school of thought that insisted that his access to prominent figures in the worlds of business and politics owed rather more to his high profile in the world of sport. Some ten years previously, Clark had given HM The Queen his Group One winning filly- Rippengal, after her racing career had finished, and Her Majesty went on to breed two Royal Ascot winners from her. Clark had also often been seen sitting in the Carrow Road Directors' box with Ed Balls when he was Economic Secretary to the Treasury. Balls was well known for being a Norwich City supporter, had been seen far less frequently at the ground after his political career had ended at the 2015 General Election – but by this time Tony Clark had established some strong relationships with some of the most influential people in the Civil Service, and so it followed naturally that successive Government Ministers would confide in him, and seek his advice on matters related to sustainable energy policy. In fact, Tony Clark had become very much a government 'insider,' which explained his presence in one of Tokyo's most exclusive hotels – but it was a privilege that he never took for granted.

After he had unpacked his suitcase and with great relief, he unfastened the belt that had been tight around his girth. He removed his trousers and reached for two miniature bottles of scotch from the room's minibar. Having also emptied the contents of a bag of peanuts into the ample palm of his left hand, he settled down in an armchair. His chicken-white legs contrasting with the deep, navy blue colour of his socks and boxer shorts, and examined the scrawled list of names that he was intending to meet the next day.

At the top of that list was the name of Richard Bryce - Fairbrother.

* * * * *

Richard Bryce-Fairbrother was the perennial favourite of government ministers – and his prominence as a leading adviser on all matters relating to economic policy were not solely due to his good looks, and easy well-spoken manner. At Harrow School, he not only broke most of the school's batting records during the cricket season, but was also regarded as something of a prodigy academically. Having graduated from Oxford University with a First-Class degree in Philosophy, Politics and Economics, the world was at his feet, and he could have excelled in any walk of life that he chose: politics, finance, academia or even the Church, as he might have followed in the footsteps of his Father, who was, at the time of the Kyoto Summit, the Bishop of Bristol.

For now, Bryce-Fairbrother was content to write his books on economics, and to nurture a developing media career. At the age of thirty-five, he was already one of the most recognised faces on British television, as an economics 'pundit,' and he had rather disdainfully turned down several lucrative offers to appear as a panel member on the nation's growing battery of reality

TV shows. He also had a particular interest in his collection of some twenty classic British sports cars, and in his ownership of a number of vineyards scattered throughout continental Europe – but the chief source of income that fed this extravagant lifestyle was his portfolio of industrial holdings, which cemented his position as a very important player in the eyes of those who manipulated the levers of power in Westminster.

Bryce-Fairbrother took a sip of champagne, as he reclined on a sofa that gave him a perfect view of the Tokyo skyline. His vantage point was the large, semi-panoramic window of Room 1219-20 of the Cerulean Tower Hotel – this was the Executive Suite, naturally. Having arrived the previous evening, he had had a hectic, but productive day of meetings with a variety of politicians, investors, and journalists. Now, at last he could relax for a few hours. His smartphone was switched to silent mode, and his A4-sized appointment book and all documents relating to the summit were stashed out of sight, and out of mind, in a large drawer in the desk that was situated at the other end of the spacious suite.

His thoughts were trained on the next important decision that he had to make – whether to take a shower or have an invigorating dip in the hotel's indoor heated swimming pool. The pool was beginning to win the internal argument when Bryce-Fairbrother's hard-earned peace was interrupted by the insistent vibrating of his smartphone, which he had idly placed on the glass coffee table, to his right. He considered ignoring the phone completely, but a combination of deep-seated conscientiousness, which compelled him to always be available to accept and respond to messages, and downright curiosity had caused him to transfer the glass of champagne into his left hand and pick up the phone.

A languid and practised sweep of the thumb revealed that a text message had arrived from a 'Tony Clark.' "Tony Clark? A common name," he thought. There must be many Tony Clark's in the world – but the name certainly had some resonance with Bryce-Fairbrother. On opening the text, Clark's opening reference to the seminar in Milan reminded the young economist that the two men had indeed met a few weeks earlier. Bryce-Fairbrother now remembered the conversation that the two men had over lunch, during which he had become slightly impatient with Clark's refusal to acknowledge the challenges presented by a large-scale conversion to wind-based energy. Nevertheless, he had been impressed with the man's passion for the subject area, and for his beloved football club. So he had agreed to meet with Clark in Tokyo, with Clark promising to show him plans and projections that would 'knock his socks off.'

Bryce-Fairbrother smiled as he remembered how many pastries Clark was able to consume, but still present a coherent argument, (albeit economically flawed, in his view), to support his ambitious plans for his new stadium. The large piece of white icing attached to Clark's lower lip, during this conversation, had proved to be something of an eye-magnet – yet it had contributed to the encounter with the entrepreneur being one that Bryce-Fairbrother was unlikely to forget.

With a great economy of words and effort, he idly hurried off a response – "Okay 10am tomoz it is" – and tossed the phone onto the luxuriously covered bed. Wearily, he rose and started on the long trek across the room to the spacious bathroom – only to be halted by an unexpected knock at the door.

"Yes?" he enquired.

There was no answer, but after a second or two, the nervous and slightly reticent knocking at the door was repeated.

"Hello?" he enquired, once again – but he had by this time resigned himself to having to go and open the door, to see for himself.

As the door swung open, Bryce-Fairbrother was greeted by the sight of a diminutive, slightly waif-like woman. She was dressed in duck egg blue summer blouse and tight-fitting, knee-length, beige denims. Her short hairstyle was rather boyish, for Bryce- Fairbrother's elegant tastes – but he felt that the young woman before him was no less attractive for that.

"Hellooo," he said, in a rich, deep voice that betrayed both surprise and interest.

"Hello. Professor Bryce-Fairbrother?" asked the woman, struggling to provide a convincing pronunciation of the name, with her Italian accent.

"Yes."

"You may not remember me, but my name is Grazia Rossini, and we met very briefly at a seminar in Milan recently. You very kindly agreed for me to interview you for my magazine, this week – I am sorry if I have caught you at an awkward time, but my editor has brought forward the deadline for the article, so would it be possible to have a few minutes of your time now?"

"I was about to take a shower, but -" One look into Grazia's innocent and pleading brown eyes was enough to persuade Bryce-Fairbrother that showering could wait, for the time being. "Yes, of course. Editors, eh? I always think of editors and journalists as being professional liars!" he quipped. Grazia's slightly confused, but otherwise blank, expression suggested to him that Ms Rossini did not quite comprehend his very English sense of humour, so slightly embarrassed, he felt he had no choice but to move the conversation on by inviting the young woman into his suite.

"Mille grazie, Professor," she said, as she sheepishly stepped over the threshold, looking around at the plush splendour of the hotel's Executive Suite.

Just as Bryce-Fairbrother was about to close the door behind her, Grazia held up her petite palm, and said: "Er, would it be possible to leave the door open? It is a protocol that I have to follow when conducting an interview alone."

"Yes, of course," replied the economist, recognising that he was in a very weak bargaining position on this issue. "A young man needs to protect himself, these days, doesn't he?" (He couldn't resist the quip – and this time he was rewarded with a shy smile).

"Where would you like to sit, Miss Rossini?"

Grazia glanced at the choice of expensive furniture that Bryce-Fairbrother had very casually offered her – and sat down, notebook in hand in the one armchair that would ensure that her interviewee was obliged to sit with his back to the door if he was to sit opposite her. Bryce-Fairbrother was of course completely unaware of the figure dressed in a white suit and wearing a white broad-brimmed panama hat, who was waiting in the corridor.

Grazia's interview with the economist lasted for a matter of seconds, before Merisi slipped silently into the suite and placed a white cotton handkerchief over Bryce-Fairbrother's nose and mouth. The entire intervention was very swift, and Merisi was now smiling at the waif-like figure who was seated with her reporter's notebook resting on her crossed legs in front of him. "Thank you, my dear. That was perfect!" he declared.

Grazia smiled back at him in a slightly shy manner. "So, what happens now?" she asked.

"Quite simply, I become Professor Richard Bryce-Fairbrother – for as long as is necessary."

"And what about him – the real Bryce-Fairbrother?" asked Grazia, pointing her chin in the direction of the man in front of her, who was slumped, open-mouthed, in a deep state of unconsciousness.

"He will be fine. I just need to put him somewhere out of sight for a day or so. When he awakes, he will be fine – except that he will have an acute bout of amnesia as to what he is about to say over the next forty-eight hours!"

"Won't he suspect that something is wrong once he discovers he has said and done things about which he has no recollection?"

"'Suspect'?" repeated Merisi. "He will certainly be confused – but I doubt very much that he will suspect that he has been impersonated by a shapeshifting, time-travelling agent from the 22nd Century. Which is fortunate!"

"Fascinating!" exclaimed Grazia, shrugging her shoulders and beaming expectantly, like a five-year-old on the morning of her birthday.

"Well, I don't wish to disappoint you, my dear, but I will not allow you to stay to witness the procedure!"

Grazia's shoulders dropped, and she contorted her face into an exaggerated frown of disappointment – but Merisi's raised index finger assured her that his decision was certainly not negotiable. "And what happens when the Room Service Manager walks in when you are half-way through your procedure?" she asked.

"That particular member of the hotel's staff is also taking an extended nap," said Merisi, in answer to Grazia's question, although he was now looking around Bryce-Fairbrother's suite, as if searching for something.

"Aha! Ecco!" he said, as he spotted the smartphone that Bryce-Fairbrother had tossed onto the bed. Merisi was pleased to discover that the phone had not been switched off, which saved him the trouble of having to over-ride the password security system that was to him rather archaic. Soon he was able to read the text message that Bryce-Fairbrother had recently sent to Tony Clark. "Excellent," he said, "the meeting with Clark is confirmed for Ten o'clock, tomorrow morning."

Merisi looked over at Grazia with an expression of quiet satisfaction and gratitude.

"You have been a great help to me, once again," he said, "but now you must leave things to me. I will see you at the summit – but, of course, by then I will have the appearance of this handsome young man here."

There was a silence as they both paused to observe the seemingly lifeless figure of Richard Bryce-Fairbrother.

Grazia was the next to speak: "I can scarcely believe the things that have happened to me, and the things that I have witnessed over the past few days," she mused.

"Yes, I can imagine that it has all been very surreal for you – to say the least. But recent events are as nothing compared to the mindless mayhem that is about to happen in Earth's future. There are still some from my time who believe that the disasters that we have seen are inevitable, and that the course of history cannot be changed. But I am certain that is not the case."

Grazia gazed out of the large window and contemplated the panoramic view of the Tokyo skyline. The sun was already casting a golden glow on the glass of the tallest buildings as early evening approached.

"Do you think everything is going to be alright?" she asked. "If you are asking me about whether the world has a future, then the answer is 'yes,' you have to have a belief that people like Dr Richards is capable of saving our world," replied Merisi – although he guessed that Grazia's thoughts were at that moment turned towards the fate of Ben Richards. "And," he added, "I have already told you that Dr Richards is in very safe hands, and that you will see him again before long. It was his destiny to go to the future and see for his own eyes the destruction caused, if we choose to take the wrong path for our future."

"Merisi, don't you get the feeling *there is a reason why*

we find ourselves in a certain place, at a certain time, to pick up certain ideas and messages along the way, that we are meant to use when we need to use them, in later life?"

"Definitely, yes Grazia. Everything happens for a reason. It is like your own personal calling. Let me tell you…

> *A belief is something you hold,*
> *The environment is something that holds you,*
> *If the environment is not held with your correct*
> *belief, then how can it hold you?*

Everyone must share the correct belief in the environment for it to hold all of us."

With a great deal of effort and gazing down at the notebook that was still in her hands, Grazia forced a smile, which was meant to show Merisi that she was reassured – but it rather took the form of a concerned grimace.

"And," added Merisi, "you may find that, rather like me, Dr Richards will appear to be a changed man!"

Grazia looked up at Merisi, unable to contemplate what the white-suited man had meant by that – but Merisi had no time to explain.

"But you need to go now," he said, placing Bryce-Fairbrother's phone in his jacket pocket, "as I have many important things to do."

With an unexpected gesture of affection, Grazia got to her feet and threw her arms around Merisi. Then, without a further word she left the room, leaving the door half-closed behind her. She walked at a steady pace along the short corridor that led to the lift – but her anxiety about what might happen in the future was gradually being overtaken by an acute sense of curiosity as to precisely what might take place in the room, that she had just left. Grazia stopped and listened, and then as if driven by a force that she could not control, turned and softly began to retrace her steps in the direction of the Executive Suite. As she looked up, she saw the figure of Merisi standing in the doorway with his usually stern and care-worn face, now wearing an expression of mock admonishment.

"Good night, my dear!" he said.

CHAPTER 6

ROOM 1001

Tony Clarke adjusted his tie as he stopped in front of his destination – Room 1001 of the Cerulean Tower Hotel. He raised his right hand, as if to knock on the oak panelled door, but then hesitated, and fumbled for the business card that she – that raven- haired beauty – had given to him. His heart pounded a little faster as he re-read the word 'masseuse' on the printed side of the card. He then double-checked the time of his informal 'appointment' and the room number, which had both been penned with an unmistakably continental hand on the reverse of the card. As he already knew, the appointed location was indeed room 1658 – and he was now ten minutes late.

As he reached forward to rap his knuckles on the oak panel, the door swung open. There in front of him, was a sight to behold. The very essence of Mediterranean, raven-haired beauty. As when Clark first gazed upon her at the seminar in Milan, what little clothing the feline seductress was wearing was entirely black, but this time the figure-hugging dress was replaced by a short silk dressing gown that was loosely secured by a bow that rested on her left hip. No other item of clothing was visible...

The woman smiled as Clark looked her up and down. "Tony, you are late!" she said, wagging her left index finger in mock admonishment.

It was then that Clark noticed the deep, blood-red colour of the woman's lipstick, before once again losing himself in the deep brown of her eyes, which had so captivated him from the first instant of their previous meeting.

After a silent pause, the woman grabbed him by his tie and hauled him into the room: "Well, you cannot stand in the corridor all evening," she said, with a sigh that feigned impatience.

As he half-tumbled into the room, Clark felt a soft pair of hands in the small of his back, guiding him to a professional-looking massage table. It was of the type that he had ordered for the Norwich City fitness suite, some six months ago, with a padded hole provided for the client's face to ensure that they could lie completely flat on the table. The only difference he noted was that the table in the room was upholstered in a subtle shade of pink, instead of the canary yellow of the football club's equipment. By the side of the massage table was a large glass of red wine, a red rose in a very slim glass vase, and a plate of heavily sugared doughnuts arranged in a neat pyramid.

"You've thought of everything!" he beamed. But the sultry masseuse was already removing Clark's clothing with the speed, stealth and silent dexterity of a pickpocket. Before he really knew what was happening, the entrepreneur was standing in the hotel room wearing nothing but his yellow and green candy-striped boxer shorts.

"Table!" demanded the masseuse, again using the palm of both hands to slap Clark in the middle of his back, coercing him in the direction of the massage table. He was slightly uncertain about the tone of domination in the woman's voice, as he had never dabbled with thoughts of masochism. Nevertheless, he needed little persuasion to climb onto the table, with his head and both chins planted firmly into the oval hole provided.

Clark waited expectantly, observing the plush carpet beneath the table. He mused briefly at the way in which its powder blue colour complemented the shades of grey of the leather suite that he could see in the corner of his eye – before his attention was diverted to the sight of a black silk dressing gown falling silently to the floor.

The next thing that Clark was aware of was the gentle weight of smooth legs on the back of his hairy rather flabby thighs, and then the softness of the skilled hands of the masseuse kneading the flesh around his lower back. He smiled and let out a long satisfied sigh.

"That's nice," he said, his mind barely registering the sound of four sharp raps on the solid wooden door.

"That's go – o – od," said the woman, as her warm hands slowly worked their way up towards Clark's shoulder blades. "Tony..." she said, in an enquiring tone of voice.

"Yes?"

"What did you do to Doctor Ree – chards?"

The question took Clark completely by surprise: "What?" he muttered and let out a yelp of pain as he felt the nails of the woman's hand penetrate between his ribs, like cold steel.

"Did you keel Doctor Ree – chards?" demanded the woman, more forcefully this time, grabbing the back of Clark's neck with her other hand.

Clark tried to raise himself from the table desperately, but he was unable to move his limbs which felt strangely leaden. As the weight of the woman on his neck increased, and with his situation apparently hopeless he summoned all his energy and let out a yell – and suddenly, he was awake and alone in his hotel room.

* * * * *

It was a very apologetic and dishevelled sight that greeted Merisi when Tony Clark eventually opened the door to his room. He had fallen asleep in his boxer shorts and vest and would have been in a deep slumber for several hours if the knock at the door had not aroused him. He had hurriedly brushed the salt and the bits of husk off his boxers – the remnants of a packet of dry roasted nuts – and grabbed a light silk dressing-gown from near the top of his open, but not yet unpacked suitcase. The silk gown mitigated the entrepreneur's embarrassment to some extent – he resolved to act as though he was just about to take a shower – but his bleary-eyed expression and the tuft of hair that was sticking straight up in the air, at the back of his head, made it obvious that he had been awake for a matter of seconds.

"Ah! Mr Clark!" said Merisi, in a perfectly honed English accent.

"Professor Bryce-Fairbrother. It's good to see you!" replied Clark, extending a podgy, but friendly hand. "I'm afraid that I was just about to..." he began gesturing towards his fairly relaxed attire – but it was a sentence that did not need completing, as Merisi was not in the least taken aback by the man's appearance. Indeed, throughout his career, he had seen far more shocking sights than that of the obese middle-aged Englishman who stood before him. Particularly during his assignment in early 17th century Italy, when he accompanied Michelangelo Caravaggio himself on tours of Rome's bordellos and taverns, which sometimes extended into weeks, rather than days. Merisi briefly reflected on how the real Richard Bryce-Fairbrother might have reacted to being greeted by Clark in such a manner – but decided that it was better to move swiftly to the job in hand, since there was no necessity for him to do anything to persuade Clark that he was Bryce-Fairbrother, given that he had shapeshifted into a hundred percent identical copy of the economist.

"No matter," he said, with a dismissive wave of the hand. "Let's keep things informal," he added, drawing Clark's attention with a laconic hand gesture, to the fact that he was dressed casually in a pair of beige cargo trousers and a blue T-shirt, which was made to look fashionable by having the logo of one of the more expensive sports brands emblazoned on one arm.

Suitably at ease, Tony Clark invited Merisi into his room – fairly spacious, mid-range accommodation for that standard of hotel, albeit fairly modest in comparison with Bryce-Fairbrother's Executive Suite. After making them both a drink from the room's well-stocked minibar – with Merisi joining his host for simplicity in having a large scotch – and having completed the formalities of 'small talk' about the rush-hour traffic in Tokyo and the views of the city from the upper floors of the hotel, Tony Clark decided it was time to broach the subject of sustainable energy generation. "I am very grateful to you for taking the time to come and see me," he began. "I understand that you have always been a strong advocate of nuclear power, Professor, but I am increasingly becoming convinced that there may be far more sustainable, and ultimately more cost-effective solutions."

"That is indeed true, but I am always very receptive to the ideas of others – and I would never be afraid to change my views completely, if there were sound economic and scientific reasons for doing so," replied Merisi, who was immediately fully engaged in the task of ensuring that the conversation should follow the course that he desired, and produce the outcomes that the UNA's teams of analysts had poured copious resources into designing. Clark was encouraged not to mention taken aback by Bryce-Fairbrother's apparent open-mindedness – and so he pressed on with making his case: "I have to say that I am becoming increasingly alarmed at some of the things I've been reading, about how much the nuclear industry is likely to cost the UK in the long run, and of course there is always the prospect of something going horribly wrong with one of the huge reactors." Merisi nodded slowly in agreement. "And, at the same time," continued Clark, "there are advancements being made in the wind generation sector in terms of efficiency and cost, which can offer us a real sustainable alternative."

Clark paused as he stared into his scotch. "And do you know who finally convinced me of this?" he asked. "Dr Ben Richards," said Clark, without waiting for an answer to his rhetorical question, "the young man who we both would have met at the Milan seminar. A talented young man who is now sadly, no longer with us."

"Yes, I understand he has been reported missing," added Merisi, "so there is, yet hope he may be found." Merisi was careful not to betray having too much knowledge – but such was Clark's obvious distress at the apparent loss of the young scientist and engineer, that he felt compelled to offer him some hope.

Tony Clark shrugged his ample shoulders in a gesture of resignation. "Maybe," he said, "but these 'missing person' cases rarely end with a 'good news' story. I fear for the young man. But - who would wish someone like that any harm?"

He rose from his seat on the sofa and paced over to the large window that looked out onto the Tokyo skyline with both hands behind his back, but with one still clutching the glass that contained his scotch. He stood staring pensively across the city for several seconds, before adding: "Of course, you yourself might be a suspect, if it turns out that Ben Richards was 'eliminated' in some way – what with you being famous for being one of the government's chief advisers on the nuclear power industry…" As he spoke, Clark offered his guest a slightly sheepish smile, as if to confirm that he was not being entirely serious with the suggestion. He was a skilled exponent of the use of the 'serious joke' as a technique for making what might be a fairly offensive suggestion, without running the risk of actually offending anyone. It was a ruse that he had often used during business negotiations, usually to test the boundaries of a prospective deal – and he was slightly surprised to find, after he had turned around to face Bryce-Fairbrother, that the remark had drawn no reaction from the economist. Instead, Merisi ignored the suggestion and returned the subject of the conversation to the issue of economics. "Yes, Dr Richards' presentation in Milan was very interesting, and I felt fairly convincing," he said.

Tony Clark again raised his eyebrows with surprise, as he once again had the impression that he might be 'pushing at an open door.'

"Of course," continued Merisi, "it is the Heads of Government who need to be convinced, especially with the economic arguments."

"Agreed!" declared Clark, with renewed vigour, and raising an index finger in order to emphasise this point. "The cost analysis is the key to making the project happen… the missing jigsaw piece. And I firmly believe that it is the financial aspects of Ben Richards' vision that are the most important innovation of all. His idea is to make use of existing roof-mounted wind turbines which are currently performing well, and extend their functionality by installing them on the roofs of stadiums. This will enable companies that have a problem with cash flow to generate their own energy, store some of it for later use and maybe even sell electricity on to the National Grid. In fact, I've calculated that the pay-back period for a large roof-mounted turbine array with energy storage, could be as little as three years instead of twelve years, which it is now."

Merisi said very little as he patiently listened to Tony Clark's economic presentation. He was fascinated at how a man whose general demeanour had previously appeared to be so inert and sluggish, could suddenly become so animated and enthused. Merisi watched as the over-weight entrepreneur darted between his suitcase and a briefcase that was left open on a table on the other side of the hotel room, pulling out engineering plans and research papers, to emphasise and re-emphasise the certainty of his argument.

As Clark picked up a detailed drawing of a roof-mounted turbine from the low coffee table that sat between the two men, he exposed the research paper beneath it. It was the paper written by Ben Richards, which Clark had used to begin his argument. The name 'Dr B. A. Richards' leapt out at Merisi. "What is important," he said, before the entrepreneur could launch into an exposition of his understanding of the engineering advantages of the turbines, "is that you take forward the work that Ben Richards began. And there must be an emphasis on using roof-mounted power generation as a means of addressing the shortage of power in urban areas. It is the most cost-effective solution that is available. That is something that Dr Richards was able to convince me of."

Again, Clark was amazed at the strength of the support that he was receiving from Bryce-Fairbrother, but so enthused was he with thoughts of what he might achieve with such an authoritative ally that he barely paused to contemplate the reasons for the economist's apparent U-turn. "Yes, of course," he exclaimed.

"It is a great pity that Ben cannot be here to champion his own ideas, but whatever his fate, I am determined to see that all his passion and his hard work will not have been in vain. I will back him to the hilt with my own resources, and those of my close business associates – which is a considerable resource – and I am confident that together we can persuade those with influence in government circles throughout the world, that sustainable energy generation of this type is the way forward. And of course, we must all hold on to the hope that he will be found, and that he can continue to lead research in this area."

Satisfied that the 'baton' was firmly in Clark's hands, and that he was as committed to the cause of roof-mounted wind turbines as could be hoped for, Merisi nodded his agreement, and settled back in the beige leather chair to hear the rest of what the man had to say. Again, Merisi listened attentively with patience, but in truth his sharpe mind was already focused on what he had to achieve the following day.

CHAPTER 7

THE BEAUTY OF THE IDEA

Ben Richards stepped out of the shower. He barely noticed that the steady flow of water from the roof of the glass cubicle ceased automatically as soon as he left it. He was also oblivious to the gentle purr of the mechanism that retrieved, and then recycled, the droplets that were left on the base, and of the sides of the shower. Six months and twenty-four days after his arrival at the UNA's rehabilitation and retraining establishment, Richards had by now, become used to the every-day 22nd century innovations that surrounded him.

One thing that he was not fully aware of however, was that his exposure to the technology of 2112 had been carefully controlled by the UNA programme managers. With the core objective of sending the scientist and engineer back almost one hundred years in time, there was some scientific knowledge that might have been downright dangerous – even in the hands, or at least the head of a well-intentioned and conscientious soul such as Ben Richards. Enabling an experienced, disciplined and well-trained operative such as Merisi to engage with civilisations at vastly different stages of development was one thing – equipping a civilian with knowledge that was a century in advance of his own time was quite another.

This very policy issue was the subject of much debate within the Authority, prior to the ultimate decision to invoke 'Operation Reset,' being made. Richards would have been astonished had he known the extent to which he had been the focus of attention in the corridors of power in the months and years leading up to the Emergency Meeting of the UNA in February 2112. Intensive research had been carried out by the scientific community into his life, his work, his family and everyone that he was known to have met during his short lifetime. The politicians and strategists at the UNA were initially at loggerheads as to the wisdom of interfering with past events. Then, when the argument against, and the viable alternatives to, Operation Reset dwindled, the discourse became focused on just how much knowledge and training and science it was necessary, and safe to provide to the trainee. The principle followed was that the transformation of Ben Richards should be minimised. He was to possess the skills, knowledge and personality traits that were necessary to enable him to realise the potential of his sustainable energy generation ideas – and so, quite literally, resurrect the career that was so suddenly ended by his untimely death in 2017. However, the senior statesmen who comprised the authoritative Ethics and Consequences Committee who were entrusted with controlling the use of the network of known time portals, were acutely aware of the dangers of certain very sensitive items of knowledge making the trip back in time. In the wrong hands, such knowledge might have consequences that would create a future far worse than the one that they were trying to eradicate.

Once the boundaries of what Richards was permitted to know had been established, enforcement of the committee's decision was a fairly straight forward process. The trainee was not permitted to leave the compound – and to do so would in any case given the extreme temperatures in Australasia at that time, and the concentration of pollutants in the atmosphere, have been fatal – and he was to engage solely with Agent Argonne, who could be programmed to divulge the precise amount of information that was necessary for any given situation.

Of course, there were times when Richards' eager and

fertile mind compelled him to bombard Argonne with endless questions about the technological innovations of the time, and of the historical events that had led to the downfall of civilisation – but such was the meticulousness of UNA's training of their agent, that as soon as a question or a response came close to the limits of what the Committee had decided that he should be permitted to know, Argonne deftly changed the subject, or gave Richards a smile that was designed to gently inform him that the subject was now closed.

It was a smile with which Richards became all too familiar, and one that he thought he recognised from his mother's face. The kindly smile that assured him that there were some things that he simply would not understand, and that she could not answer all of his many questions. "Surely, they haven't been able to reproduce my mother's smile, have they?" he once asked himself. This was added to the inventory of unanswered questions.

During the early weeks of his rehabilitation and training, Richards exercised his mind by trying to deduce answers to his questions on the basis of what Argonne had NOT said. But, before long he formed the distinct impression that his sole companion was wise to that tactic. In fact, he soon came to the conclusion that his attempts to out-manoeuvre or outwit his trainer were as futile as those of a chess novice striving to defeat a Grand Master – and so the questions eventually stopped, and he buckled down to his training.

The only times when Argonne's serene competence appeared to waver slightly were when Richards began to ask her questions about the prosthetic reparations that had been made to his legs, which had been damaged seemingly beyond repair during the attack by Feng. Evidently, providing him with new lower limbs, and his subsequent recovery were not part of UNA's plan. Several times Richards asked Argonne about the science and the rationale behind the procedures that he had undergone. Apart from having an academic curiosity, he was understandably keen to know precisely what materials and biomechanics had been incorporated into his body. At such times, Argonne began to provide an explanation – only to hesitate, pause for a second's contemplation, and then give him that 'mother's smile.'

What was plainly obvious to Richards was that his new legs were far superior to the ones he had when he passed through the portal. They were **stronger.** He could run much faster, and fatigue was barely an issue at all. He had always been a keen athlete, and had always tried to keep himself fit, but his performance levels during the physical training that Argonne put him through were truly astounding. In fact, the only physical limitation he seemed to have, was the rate at which his lungs could consume sufficient oxygen to fuel his exertions.

Yet, the advanced prosthetics certainly looked and felt like his own legs. Once the skin had regrown – which happened remarkably quickly – they were an exact replica of the ones that he had known all his life. There were moles and veins in all the same places. The only differences were that they were 'chicken white,' lacking the tan that had become almost permanent, after thirty-odd summers of wearing shorts, and the scar caused by an unfortunate incident with a barbed wire fence when he was eight, was missing.

Needless to say, the whole experience of training and rehabilitation in a strictly controlled environment, and with an android as his sole companion was both fascinating and surreal. Very soon however, he began to feel confined and lonely, and longed for human company – and his thoughts often turned to Grazia, and her uncertain fate.

Argonne had been trained to be conversant – within strictly controlled subject guidelines, of course – and there was no doubting her beauty. She had been crafted with features that had a flawless elegance – rather like a fashion designer's mannequin. Her body was of course, a vision of athletic perfection. Richards could not help noticing the perfection of her thighs and of her posterior – yet, throughout the entire duration of his time with her, he never experienced a glimmer of sexual desire towards her. "That's something else that they can somehow control!" he once thought to himself.

But overall, the days, and weeks, and months passed by peacefully and without stress. His surroundings were pleasant, all of his physical and nutritional needs were catered for, and the gardens beyond the bubble of his temporary environment were constantly bathed in bright, albeit lethal sunshine.

A feature of his rehabilitation and training was a varied, but utterly predictable routine. At precisely the same time every morning after he had showered and enjoyed a pre-prepared breakfast, he would proceed to a training suite where he would find Argonne standing, ready to begin the day's programme – always with the same upright posture and welcoming smile. One day however, there was a noticeable change to the routine. It was a Friday. Fridays normally began with two hours of hand- to-hand combat training – but on this occasion, Argonne did not wait for Richards in the training suite. Instead, she entered his quarters as soon as he had finished his breakfast of granola and cherry yoghurt. Ben knew that something must be afoot!

"Good morning Dr Richards," said Argonne.

"Everything perfectly normal so far then," thought Richards to himself, nodding slightly in response. But then Argonne got straight to the point.

"Shui Feng has been located," reported the android, at which point Richards experienced vivid flashbacks of his previous encounter with GIATCOM's most advanced, and most ruthless, asset. "We have detected his presence in the vicinity of Qiandao Lake," continued Argonne, "which is 350-kilometres south-west of Shanghai, at precisely 14.22pm on August 22nd, 2017. This is a man-made lake, which was created as part of a hydroelectric power project – and our analysts are connecting his presence with contemporary rumours of the 'lost city of Shi Cheng,' the ruins of which it was believed, were submerged when the lake was created."

Argonne paused, having delivered her initial message. Richards was unable to fill the silence as he contemplated what this news might mean for his immediate future. Having undergone months of fairly intense training, he was excited at the prospect of finally having the opportunity to put his new skills – and his new improved limbs – to the test, but he was nonetheless apprehensive at the thought that he might have to renew his acquaintance with Shui Feng. He only had a few seconds to wait before his long-time companion confirmed his worst fears.

"You will leave for Shanghai in 2017 to rendezvous with our agents there, immediately."

"And......... what about the summit in Tokyo? Isn't that supposed to be my main objective?" asked Richards.

"Shanghai is your next objective," replied Argonne coldly, but with an emphasis that confirmed to Richards that the plan was non-negotiable. "You will need to pass through the time portal to 2017 in any case – as planned – but your itinerary has now changed, so that you will first complete your mission at Qiandao Lake."

"Mission?"

"Everything will be explained to you in good time."

Argonne relayed the information with her usual reassuring clarity and certainty – and ended the interaction with a smile that Richards had come to understand to be the one that she was programmed to display in order to give him the 'trust me – everything will be fine' message. But Richards wasn't absolutely sure, on this occasion.

"And this is a mission for me, is it?" he asked, with eyebrows slightly raised.

Argonne immediately recognised his expression of uncertainty and understood his self-doubt. "Yes," she replied. "You are wondering why we do not send an android to perform the task."

Richards didn't bother to reply. He had learnt, months ago, that Argonne's interpretation of his facial expressions was invariably hundred percent accurate, and that her advanced programming had made her virtually telepathic.

"The reason for sending you to perform the task," she continued, with barely a moment's hesitation, "is that your presence by the lakeside is the last thing that Feng will suspect. He will be alert to the appearance of one of the UNA's androids, but he will not even be aware that you are still alive. He will certainly have no knowledge of your newly acquired capabilities – and I can assure you that you now have everything you need in order to complete your mission."

Richards, paused for thought as he gazed into Argonne's

eyes.

"You see, Doctor, put this Virtual Reality headset on and you will see how your perception can be corrected. The imagery can unblock your negative perception of an event caused by your memory of a trauma and reveal a different, more positive way of perceiving a previous event in your memory or an event you are about to encounter. Switch this on; by clicking this switch at the back of your neck, it taps into your mind and gives you a positive thought release, whist giving you a holistic picture of an event from different perspectives. It's named the **Gestalt switch**. It manipulates your brain rhythm whilst you see the imagery, allowing you to process the information in a different way to see the whole picture. **Allowing you to see- the sum of all the parts, not just the part you are fixated on and want to see.** It underpins the gestalt theory of perception. Things happen for a reason and in order to know fully why things happen. You need **to understand the big picture and perceive all the parts that make up that event in time.** Your personal perception of an event may not see the whole full true perception of an event. **Sometimes there is nothing you can do to change a situation, what happens is circumstance.** By using this Virtual Reality (VR) headset, you can now replay a memory of an event you experienced and understand the whole event. You can use this VR to understand the true meaning of why your mother thought you were waving from the shore, and how she was unaware of a big tidal wave approaching her."

Richards subdued with the information provided by Argonne, nodded and then smiled, acknowledging that he had at last the technological answer to help him break free from his PTSD.

"Given the fact that the whole of your left leg and arm severely lost human tissue which left you seconds away from dying before we found you, we decided to reconstruct the whole of your body to with a cybernetic organism material which creates a bionic armour, giving you more protection and power. Its armour also offers a façade that has a vast number of capillaries that enable you to absorb oxygen from the air to maximise your oxygen intake, and store the additional oxygen intake for when you need more oxygen in polluted areas of earth at present here on Earth, or when you go back to Earth in your present."

"We have also injected into your bloodstream an advanced nano-sensor which enables you to read the thoughts of other humans, humanoids and androids. However, be aware that most of the advanced androids, such as Feng and humanoids, such as Merisi, already have this capability. However, you have a distinct advantage where you can use your human philosophical thinking to try and mind control Feng to change his attitude and behaviour and thus actions, by reading his mind before he carries out an action, and prevent his action by allowing that someone to read your mind before they make the action, and be convinced by you not to make that action. The influence of mind control acts a bit like blue tooth technology, where information can pass from one destination to another wirelessly if both nano-sensors within both beings are live. Or you can simply just read other humans' minds before they make their actions and counteract their actions more responsively in advance of their actions. The nano-sensor technology works by tapping into the electrical signals that neurons use to send information to each other. The exchange of sensory information happens when humans, androids, humanoids are about to carry out any action, such as; moving, thinking, or speaking. You are able to read others' minds wirelessly and convince androids and humanoids by allowing them to see your influential mind. It is not invasive, avoiding; microchip implants, surgery or wires being implanted into your body. You can hack someone's mind and access everything on it, within a range of thirty metres."

"Lastly, your DNA has been reconstructed to become genetically engineered with CRISPR as the latest form of humanoid using the latest cybernetic organism material. CRISPR is a genome editing technology that allows scientists to cut DNA with incredible precision and insert or delete DNA to correct unwanted mutations of DNA, or viruses affecting DNA."

"It's the power to edit the building blocks of life, by switching off genes that lead to a broad spectrum of disease, but it will unshackle all of us from the genetics we're born with. The incoming wave of gene editing applications was compared to the Industrial Revolution or the birth of the internet in terms of the game-changing impact it had on society. Gene editing became the new IT in the 21st century. Governing the correct ethical philosophy in design through governmental control, in a more corporate socially responsible way. The development of CRISPR Cas9 became the first gene editing tool in 2012."

"Since then, the development of CRISPR advanced to become integrated with AI to produce humanoid integrated technology through cybernetic organism tissue & AI material. At first, the integrated technology was used to fight against advanced mutations of disease in the first part of the 21st century, after a huge investment in commercial research laboratories to test and create solutions to life-threatening illness. Quality Management Systems in Virus testing control and Genome sequencing in the production of testing for illness in humans advanced to a large commercial scale. Robotic automation of androids were being used in commercial research laboratory facilities to mitigate the risk of human error and a production facility to become more productive and safer. And then..."

"And then what?" asked Richards.

"AI was used to help us survive as humans. As air pollution escalated due to climate change and a series of nuclear disasters in the latter part of the 21st century."

Then she suddenly broke into a rhyme as she moved closer to Dr Richards and stroked his hair.

"All is not what it may seem,
The blended reality from your dreams.
Look more closely without fear,
Your hidden truth will appear," the android nurse whispered in Dr Richards' ear. She continued to stroke his hair, as a way of reassuring him that his transformation is now complete.

"Look and you will find,
In the landscape to your mind,
In your foreground is the truth,
Hiding the background to your youth."

Again, Argonne concluded the delivery of the information with the 'reassurance' smile, but Richards had already averted his gaze away from her perfect features. He turned, and very slowly and thoughtfully sat down on the leather-covered bench where minutes earlier he had enjoyed breakfast with very little of concern in his head.

"You are concerned that Shui Feng might recognise you," said Argonne. Once again, her interpretation of Ben's body language was precisely accurate, and so neither confirmation nor denial was required. "Do not worry," the android continued, "for we have designed a disguise for you. You will appear at the lakeside in a full kendo master's outfit, complete with a mask. Your cover will be that of a kendo instructor, and you will be in the process of carrying out an exercise routine at the precise time that Shui Feng arrives on the scene. Kendo, as a sport and a fitness pastime was very popular in China during this time, so nobody will consider your presence there to be unnatural."

Suddenly, it occurred to Richards that there had after all been a purpose to the many hours of instruction that he had received in all styles of Japanese martial art. He had become especially proficient in the art of kendo – although it had not occurred to him, he might be required to indulge in swordplay with the likes of Shui Feng.

"It is the opportunity for **the hunted to become the hunter,"** added Argonne, in a cryptic manner that surprised Richards. "We do not know Feng's precise purpose of visiting the lake, Dr Richards, but he must be there for a reason – and we need you to find out what it is."

Richards continued to say nothing as he sat, silently contemplating his immediate future.

In the absence of further questions from her trainee, Argonne proceeded to her next instruction: "Come. There is a vehicle waiting for you outside. The portal will be opened in seventy-four minutes time."

CHAPTER 8

DEVIL IN THE PLAYGROUND

en Richards peered through the narrow slits in the full kendo mask that had been fitted to his head prior to his surprisingly brief one hundred year journey. The anti-nausea pills that he had been administered prior to his passing through the portal had ensured a seamless and efficient transition – and he had now arrived on the banks of the lake.

After completing a full charge from his on-body battery pack, his superhuman bionic limbs were now electrically charged from the solar power they were exposed to and stored within his body. He was now ready and waiting and commenced a now familiar exercise routine.

After a few minutes of swinging his bamboo sword with deft footwork he paused, raised his mask slightly, and surveyed the scene around him. He breathed in the fresh lakeside air. The climate was of course refreshingly temperate. After several months in a constant air-conditioned environment, he enjoyed the sensation of the gentle breeze across his face. The flow of air over the beads of sweat on the nape of his neck cooled him after his brief exertions in the heavy protective suit.

He appeared to have a newfound confidence as he slowed

down his sweeping action of the sword. He remembered Argonne saying, "It's like anything. **The more time you spend practicing something, the more you perfect your craft.**"

Richards surveyed the scene. He had been well briefed by a second android, after Argonne had escorted him to the waiting vehicle, of what he could expect to see on his return to 2017. Sure enough, as described, he found himself standing on the pebbly shore of a vast featureless lake. As he gazed across the water, he could just make out the thin grey outline of what he had been informed was the south-east extremity of Qiandao Lake. In the other direction there was grassland, punctuated with a few clumps of dwarf bushes. Beyond the land climbed steadily up a shallow escarpment to a vast green forest that stretched back as far as the eye could see. It occurred to Richards that this was a rare unspoilt natural vista, the like of which had long disappeared from the troubled era he had just left behind. All was still, except for the gentle swaying of the bushes in the breeze. After his comfortable but rather sterile captivity, Richards was acutely aware of the sound of birdsong in the air. But otherwise, he was satisfied that he was completely alone with no detectable evidence of human activity.

He pulled back the sleeve of his protective suit and glanced at the timepiece that UNA had given him as he embarked on his journey. If the information supplied to him were correct – and he had grown accustomed to having complete confidence in the accuracy of the UNA's intelligence – then Shui Feng would arrive at the lake in precisely fourteen minutes. He felt a strange sense of being in complete control, given the knowledge that he had been given of precisely what was about to happen during the ensuing minutes. Yet, he was filled with apprehension, with the realisation that from the appearance of Shui Feng, he would be on his own, and responsible for his own destiny. His new protectors at the UNA had no control over his immediate future. He remembered Argonne's last words to him: "Don't worry, Doctor. Your training will stand you in good stead," and there was that 'reassurance' smile, as a parting gift. Besides, he was now more equipped physically and mentally than ever. Free from his trauma, he reflected on the flashback of images he was shown by Merisi in his mind as he waited for Feng. But this time they were much more vivid with brightness, sharpness, and colour. He understood the messages from the imagery and what he needed to be aware of, and what he needed to do.

* * * * *

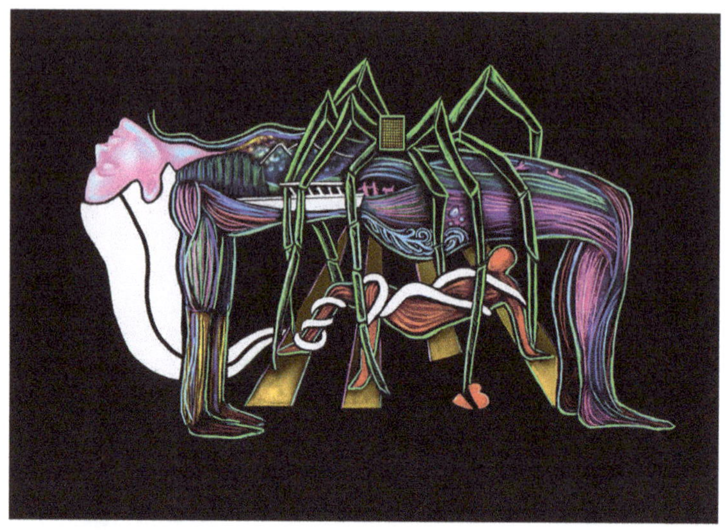

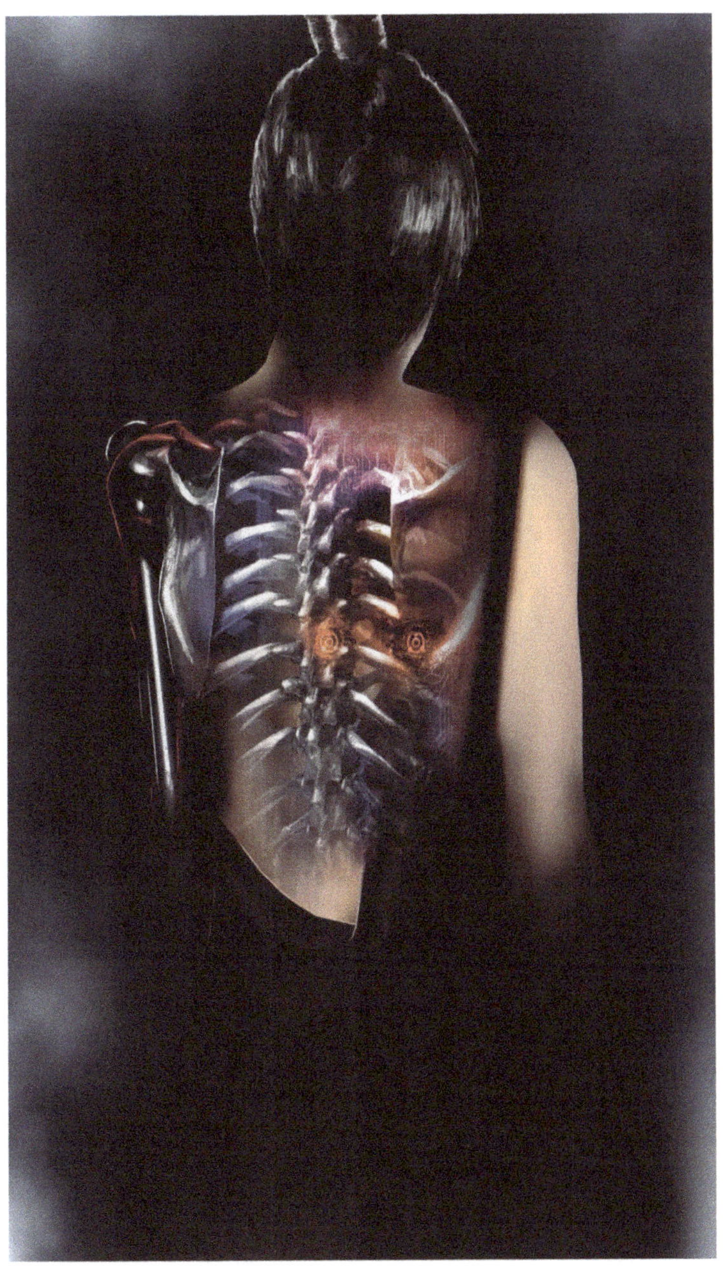

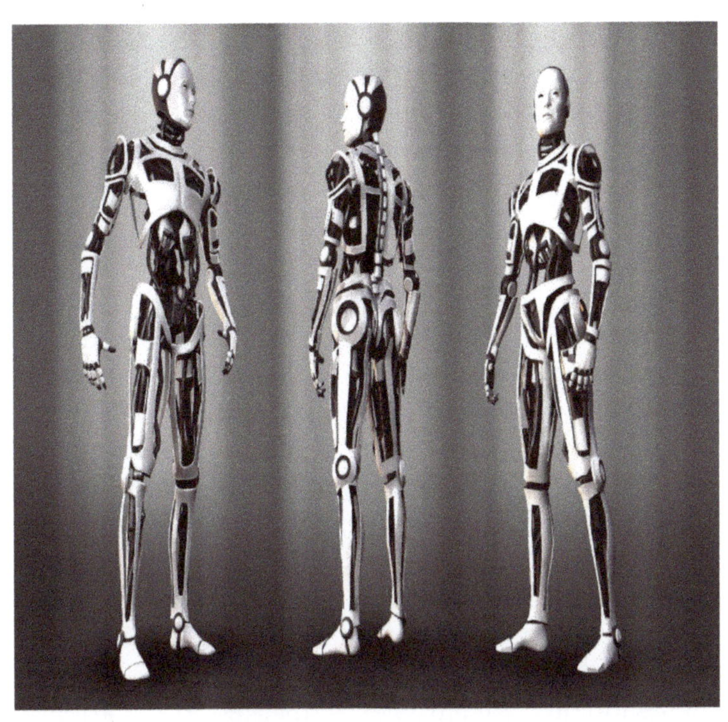

Then suddenly, he snapped out of his flashbacks and visions. Richards' final reassurance was provided by the fact that Feng appeared at the precise time that he was supposed to. "How could he not?" reasoned Richards to himself. "What I have just witnessed had already happened – but from this point onwards, nothing is certain."

In fact, as he himself realised how events were about to unfold, was totally unpredictable. What was Shui Feng about to do? How would Shui Feng react if, when he spotted the man in the samurai suit? How would Richards react in response? More importantly, to what extent was the young man ready to face the challenge that was now very near? Would the months of training, and the 22nd-century physical enhancements stand him 'in good stead,' as Argonne had assured him? What did Argonne actually mean by that?

All of these thoughts flitted through Ben Richards' mind – for precisely fourteen minutes – as he meticulously worked his way through the rehearsed kendo training routine.

Then suddenly, Richards eyes diverted to the attention of a little girl swinging her Papa's hand whilst waiting in a queue for a boat ride, somewhat thirty metres away from him near the harbour's edge. "What was that, Papa?" the little English tourist girl asked - as loud barking of a dog increased with intensity.

"Don't you hear that?" she cried.

"What?" her father snapped, witnessing terror in her eyes.

The barking ferociously intensified as the sound got closer. It came from around the corner of the side street thirty metres away from where the little girl and her father were standing in the queue, in the opposite direction from where Richards was standing.

Then suddenly – "Yelp! Yelp! Yelp!" the barking halted to a stop.

All was silent, but a breeze of wind that eerily blew past the tourists' ears.

The little girl grabbed hold of her father's hand tight, as the fear in her little face intensified.

A dark figure appeared from the corner of the side street. The figure approached the back of the queue in a stealth and industrious like manner. The queue of tourists looked at each other with despair and wariness at this uninvited character who had now joined their tour.

At the pre-set time, and without interrupting Richards' routine, the familiar figure of Shui Feng had arrived with his incomparable presence. Feng had no need for a disguise, and so had adopted what Richards assumed to be his 'natural' appearance – or at least what could pass for being 'natural' for an entirely man-made organism.

Richards was briefly struck by the irony of the artificial and malevolent figure, in the context of that innocent and unspoilt landscape, but such thoughts were soon overwhelmed by the dread that was instilled by Feng's previous shape shifting disguise as a furtive, feline full of athleticism. Here, Richards reminded himself of what was a formidable and dangerous opponent, and one with which he might shortly have to engage.

For now, however, he was content to observe Shui Feng from a relatively 'safe' distance.

One curious factor that immediately sprung to Richards' mind, was Feng alone? As he could see a few men some few hundred metres away in the background dragging a large rowing boat across some dry grey pebbles. It appeared that this group of four middle-aged Chinese men were to join the queue. All were chattering excitedly in Chinese and were heavily laden with diving equipment. These appeared to be not androids, but how could he be sure? As the disguise technology was forever evolving and advancing, so you couldn't detect completely. Richards was quickly able to guess that Feng had arrived at this location under the guise of running a commercial diving operation. He wondered how long the assassin had spent in creating this ruse – and how many innocent people had been 'eliminated' in order to provide him with the cover he needed to serve the purpose of visiting the lake. What was almost inevitable was that the day-trippers accompanying Feng had an uncertain, and probably very short future – but Richards was no nearer to discovering Feng's intentions.

Richards ceased his exercise routine and moved away from the lake shore so that he would be partially hidden from Shui

Feng's view, behind a low gently swaying bush. He watched all five figures began to don their full diving gear. Richards realised that the distraction of putting on the gear and equipment provided him with the ideal opportunity to inch closer to the group. So in spite of his fear, he crept along the shore of the lake. Ensuring all the time that he remained hidden behind a bush or a particularly well-grown clump of grasses.

By the time he had approached to within ear-shot – and he was fortunate that he was downwind of the men – all five had changed into their diving suit, except for the required headgear. By this time Richards had discarded his own helmet and mask, and was now able to clearly hear Shui Feng addressing the group. Clearly his briefing speech had been meticulously prepared.

"The 'lost city' will amaze you," he announced in a clear, confident tone. "You will witness a whole complex of white temples, memorial arches, paved roads and intricately decorated houses. Hidden some hundred and thirty feet underwater. This is China's Atlantis! It was called 'The Lion City,' and it was built in the shadow of Five Lion Mountain. Here, once was the city of Shi Cheng - the centre of politics and commerce of the eastern province of Zhejiang."

"In 1959, the Chinese government decided that a new hydroelectric power station was required, and so created this man-made lake. You can see the power station over there," said Feng, pointing to a structure that could just about be seen in the distance. "This city acquired the name Shi Cheng," he continued, "from the nearby Wushi Mountain, which became known as Wushi Island after it had become partially submerged by the lake. 'The Lion City' was built during the time of the Eastern Han Dynasty, of AD 25–200. One of the features of the city, as I explained to you all earlier, was a unique irrigation system called 'Dujiangyan.' This is a system that was used by the Qin dynasty, centuries earlier, and is the sole surviving dam-less irrigation system in the world."

Richards' contempt for the bespoke assassin was at that moment replaced by an engineer's fascination for what Feng was explaining to his diving party. Suddenly, it became clear to Richards that the four Chinese gentlemen must be businessmen

– so he sensed potential investors. But what he wondered, was Feng's interest in a group of investors? Was the hapless quartet simply a cover for Shui Feng's trip to the lake, or does he really have an interest in the development of an innovative irrigation system? The latter possibility seemed to him to be outlandish – but such was his fascination with the idea of a dam- less irrigation system that he listened on.

"Some say," continued Feng, "that the city of Shi Cheng could have used the fast-flowing spring and melt water from the Wushi mountain in order, like Dujiangyan, to create an artificial levee, and redirect a portion of the river's flow to cut a channel through the Wushi mountain. Excess water could be discharged to irrigate farmland within the region of Shi Cheng."

"This gentlemen, is a wonder of ancient Chinese science. Built over 2,200 years ago, this incredible feat of engineering could still be used today to irrigate over 668,700 hectares of farmland, drain floodwater and provide water resources for more than fifty other cities in the province. More than two millennia ago, the region in which Dujiangyan now stands was threatened by the frequent floods caused by flooding of the Minjiang River, a tributary of the Yangtze. Li Bing, a local official of Sichuan Province at that time, together with his son, discovered that the river was swelled by fast-flowing spring meltwater from the local mountains, which burst its banks when it reached the slow moving and heavily silted water downstream. One solution would have been to build a dam, but Li Bing had also been charged with keeping the waterway open for military vessels to supply troops on the frontier. So instead, he came up with his revolutionary idea."

"Li Bing's idea was to combat the problems caused in times of drought by using the surplus water from river flow in times of heavy rainfall. This is better than submerging towns and villages, or depriving a community of water by building a dam. A dam is the cure after failed prevention, rather than **prevention before the cure.** What Dujiangyan achieved was innovative thinking - and a stroke of genius!"

The diving party listened to Feng's impressive presentation in seemingly awe-struck silence – as did Richards, who had not anticipated hearing such wisdom from the killing machine that had maimed him so unfeelingly. What's more, the fact that Feng was addressing his audience in English – which was impeccable and without a trace of a foreign accent – suggested to Richards that this was no mere collection of local businessmen, but a select band of entrepreneurs drawn from all over Southeast Asia.

"A further aspect of the scheme," Feng went on, "was that the water that flowed through the Mount Yulei channel, discharged excess water to turn water wheels, which provided an additional source of power for grinding grain and other purposes. Besides the water being used to mechanically power production of food for communities, it was used for water storage and conservation for future irrigation and sanitation in times of drought."

On hearing this, Richards realised Feng's plan.

He sank down on his haunches and reflected on what he had just heard. It was clear that Shui Feng had travelled to this location to gain information – but for what purpose? He had all the appearance of being an entrepreneur rather than a cold, emotionless assassin. What were his motives? Could the android actually have 'motives,' in the human sense of the term? It was a conundrum that Richards was certainly not expecting.

The sound of water splashing drew Richards' attention back to the scene by the shore of the lake. He raised himself slightly, so that he could see above the long blades of grass that had kept him from Feng's sight. He could now see that the android's presentation had come to an end, and that he was now pushing the boat laden with the four day-trippers into the lake. Feng then leapt into the boat, with the agility and athleticism that Richards recognised all too well. This reminder of his previous encounters with the assassin caused him to think of Grazia once again. As he cautiously watched Shui Feng row the boat away from the shoreline, his thoughts were dominated by what Grazia's fate might be – or might have been. As the image of the boat became more and more distant, Richards' heart became filled with a loathing of Shui Feng, and with a feeling of helplessness in being powerless to prevent Grazia from being at the mercy of this callous brute – this unfeeling machine. He could not fathom Shui Feng's motives or intentions – but a steely determination grew within him to confront his nemesis, and to defeat him at the first opportunity.

CHAPTER 9

CLOSE ENCOUNTER

Once the small boat had diminished into the far distance, Richards had emerged from his hiding place in the long grass, and now sat on some dry pebbles, just a few yards away. He had discarded the kendo training suit. It was heavy and cumbersome, and he felt that he no longer needed the disguise as his 'cover' for being at the location. He was now fully focused on Feng and certainly had no qualms about the assassin recognising him. After the intense training that he had received over several months, rightly or wrongly, he was confident that he would be able to hold his own with the android.

* * * * *

"Ok gentlemen, prepare yourself to see the spectacle of your life… to witness seeing the incredible Chinese wonder that is… the lost underwater city of Shi Cheng."

The party of divers all sitting on the starboard of the boat, including Feng, all laid backwards whilst adjusting their scuba mouth pieces and fell into the water headfirst.

Feng was clearly on a mission with vision.

As they approached one hundred metres deep, they could see what looked like an iconic looking building like that of a church. Feng waved furiously with his arm, directing the party to follow him to go inside the building. He obviously was aware of something that he could find from his investigation.

At the back of the church was an altar which had a tabernacle object. Feng seemed to be ecstatic in seeing it, as his eyes lit up and waved more furiously to his followers to follow him to the object. It was in the shape of a three-dimensional, three foot triangular like pyramid shape with a triangular shaped base. One side of the triangle was longer than the other two sides, which were also of different length.

Feng knew he had found what he had been looking for, and frantically tried to open the small tomb encased structure from the base. He realised he had to prove his creative thinking to creatively problem solve, rather than just rely on linear programmed thought he would normally rely on as an android. He had to evolve his thinking to be able to move the base of this structure to find what he was looking for.

The party bewildered by what he was doing, began tapping on their watches, implying that they had been down long enough and needed to go back up for air!

Feng held his hand up indicating give me five minutes. The concerning thing was they only had enough air left to hold out for six minutes and in their oxygen supplies, and they had to factor in swimming backup as well.

Fright drew upon all of their faces, as Feng looked more and more determined as he looked for some sort of code to crack his puzzle of opening the tabernacle.

Then suddenly he finds to the side of the tabernacle some shapes that depicts the theory behind teaching children at that time the theory of Pythagoras' theorem.

He realises it was a puzzle game which was used to teach mathematics at that time the relationships between shapes. The space was irregular and required the shapes to be fitted in the irregular space correctly in order to open the tabernacle. He immediately went to work to figure out how these shapes fitted into the space. Identifying that the medium- and small sized square areas added together make up the total area of the large sized square which fitted into the space, creating the large side of the triangle shape situated within the irregular space. He thought, the Chinese were obviously developing similar philosophies to the Greek mathematical philosophy teachings at that time, and remembered from his mathematical training at Giatcom that Pythagoras' theorem stated - In any triangle that contains a right angle, the square on the hypotenuse (long side of the triangle) is equal to the sum of the squares on the other two sides. Within three minutes he had filled the irregular space with the shapes.

To all their amazement the tabernacle opened to reveal some hidden papers. He had cracked the code with his mathematical and logical thinking.

Feng quickly flicked his headlamp on, to see the words scribed big and bold in Chinese on the first page of these papers, and in English translate to –**"The whole is more than the sum of its parts."**

As the party including Feng reached the top of the water gasping for air, Feng clenched the papers shaking the water off them. He pulled his scuba mouthpiece out and shouted, "Yes! I have the technical plan drawings of how the ancient Chinese were going to create the first multi-purpose water powered plant, - which was a series of turbines driving flood water for; irrigation, flood defence, and grain producing."

"This is a marvel of the past, present and future, and it is in my hands!"

* * * * *

Richards now enjoyed the warmth of the rising morning sun as he gazed out across the lake. From what he could make out, the boat had stopped, and the members of the diving party were taking turns in entering the water, and then re-emerging. The activity was too distant for Richards to properly make out what was going on – so he waited, always alert to any sign that the party might be ready to return.

Time was of no relevance to Richards, but he guessed that Shui Feng and his entourage must have been on the lake for some two hours before it became obvious that the boat was heading back to the lake shore. He returned to his hiding place in the grass, and stealthily went back to where he had discarded his kendo equipment, retrieving his bamboo training staff. This would be his only protection against Shui Feng, should he have the opportunity to confront him. Argonne had explained to him, before he passed through the portal, that protocol did not permit them to supply him with 22nd century weaponry, and that in any case, his remit was to gain intelligence on what Shui Feng was doing at the lake, and not to engage with him. Richards hoped that Shui Feng had 'travelled light' in a similar fashion.

Clutching the bamboo implement, and crouched on one knee, Richards watched as Feng led the party back to the shore. Evidently the trip had been a successful one, as all appeared to be in high spirits. There were smiles and 'high fives,' as the visitors chattered away in what Richards took to be mandarin.

"So, gentlemen," declared Feng, once all had set foot on the stony shore. "We have seen the wisdom of the past – and I can promise you it will bring us all a bright and profitable future!" This statement was greeted with enthusiastic approval from those surrounding Shui Feng. "I now have all that I need in order to complete my work," added Feng, fondly tapping a package or device of some sort, that he had stashed away in his breast pocket.

Richards did not know what it was that spurred him into action at that moment. Maybe it was Shui Feng's self-satisfied smile. Maybe it was the indignation that he felt at Feng's use of the words 'my work,' when he had clearly not done any research of his own. It might just have been the realisation that Feng was about to lead his party away from the lake, but something had to compel Richards to stand up and emerge from his grassy hiding place, and advance towards the party to be able to look Shui Feng straight in the eye.

And then he remembered the story of a man he once met, which he held as the most courageous person he had met and replayed the story in his mind.

It was his best story that he had crossed his path. If he started feeling guilty about being fortunate or making the wrong decision, that didn't quite go to plan and had hung over his head it was this man's story. **A true victim of circumstance.**

He met an old guy at university where he was pitching a product invention to this man, and a team full of his associates. Afterwards he went to the toilet, and this man was only one left out of the party of people he was pitching to. The man had deliberately waited for him, to escort him out of the building. He could see he was on crutches and had only one leg.

He asked him, "How it happened?" Bearing in mind, this guy was about seventy-eight years old.

The man replied, "When I was working for the government on designing fighter planes in the cold war, I was coming out of a side street in Brussels. And suddenly boom!"

"I got ran over."

"I was in a coma for almost a year and when I eventually woke up, I found myself paralysed for life at the age of forty."

Richards thought, what a remarkable man who has spent over half his life being disabled from no fault of his own, yet inspired to live on. That's when the penny dropped, and he immediately thought your health and well-being, and **courage to live on, is far more important than just failing in life and worrying about mistakes you make or things that you cannot control.** When there are far more important things that are out of your control, which can have devastating consequences to you. When something as severe as your legs have been taken away from you, that is far worse than say money being taken away from you.

Moreover, he thought people who had seen this man for the first time like he did, have an initial judgement on him acquiring the crutches due to his old age, because he's aged at seventy-eight, unknowingly he has had them since the age of forty. You automatically assume he has only acquired his bad legs in later years. But no… this man has had this disability most of his life due to someone savagely taking his life away from him. But it didn't stop him from battling on. Richards went home, and it brought him to tears thinking about it.

It was as if the old man was his guardian angel that had come down from heaven and was trying to tell him to stop worrying about getting into debt for his investment that may not materialise, and stop feeling guilty about it. When things that are out of your control, can happen to you in life, which can be far worse.

It suddenly dawned upon him, that he was fortunate to be given the chance to use his own legs again and now was the time for him to put them to good use!

He rose and walked forward to Feng.

There was no expression of surprise on Feng's face as he detected Richards moving towards him – but he recognised the young scientist and engineer immediately.

"Ah! Dr Richards!" he said, rather in the manner of a dentist greeting his next patient. In contrast, there was amazement among his entourage, in such a remote location. They all turned and looked at Richards. There was a silence as Richards approached, before Feng added: "It seems that we have a tourist, eager for a trip out into the lake. I see that you have brought your own oar," he said, with a nod to the bamboo weapon that Richards held in his right hand, "but I don't think it will be very effective. I have something far more appropriate in the boat."

With that, Feng turned and started to walk towards the small boat that sat on the waterline, with small waves lapping gently at its sides. Richards was instantly aware of the possibility that the android might have some form of weapon stashed away in the boat, and so he moved with awesome speed and agility, and was soon standing in Feng's path, holding his bamboo cane out in front of him as a horizontal barrier.

Feng was not slow to recognise the implications of Richards' newfound physical capabilities.

"Impressive, Doctor," he said. "You are so much quicker on your feet than you were when I last saw you! I can see that the UNA must have taught you well!" Feng stretched out with an arm, intending to grab Richards by the shoulder and move him to one side – but, in no time at all, Richards had countered the move, and was now holding Feng tightly by the wrist. There was now no doubt in Feng's mind that Richards was not the same person who he had been able to deal with so easily when he wrested the ancient roman artefacts away from him. It took Feng no time at all to sum up the situation.

"I see that your new friends have been teaching you some new tricks, Doctor," declared Feng, loudly enough for his companions to hear. "It will be my pleasure to test my kendo skills with you – in another time and another place, maybe…"

"I have no intention of indulging in sport with you, Feng," replied Richards, with a firmness and a resolution that made it clear that this was no friendly encounter. "I have suffered enough pain and anguish as a result of your deeds – and I have not travelled a hundred years merely to 'joust' with you!"

There was no mistaking the menace in Richards' voice – but Feng remained calm and unmoved.

"Oh, really?" exclaimed Feng. "It seems that the Doctor," he added, turning towards the four astonished businessmen, "has delusions about time travel!"

The diving party understood the reference immediately: "Doctor Who! Doctor Who!" they cried, chuckling with amusement.

"Maybe," continued Feng, "the Doctor has forgotten which century he is in!"

This was a jolting reminder to Richards that he had to be very careful about what he said and did. Part of his UNA training had emphasised the importance of avoiding any potential 'technology shock' that might be caused by two worlds, separated by a century of scientific development coming together. Richards' training had been extremely thorough, but at this moment it was obvious to him one of them was having his thoughts and actions governed by emotion – and it was certainly not Shui Feng. Richards felt his heart beating faster and faster, and as Feng implacably held his gaze, he could not escape the feeling that the android clearly had the upper hand. But it was too late now to take a backward step. "I don't know what you're up to Feng," he continued, desperately searching in his mind, for a way forward, "but I will not let you destroy my world. I cannot let you destroy it."

Shui Feng pressed home his advantage with a confused expression that made it clear to his companions that he hadn't the faintest idea of what the young man was talking about. "'Destroy it?" he cried, with exaggerated incredulity. "Why should I destroy the world? My business partners and I are going to save the world and ensure that it has a sustainable future. What are you talking about?" Feng turned, with a smile, to his 'business partners,' with a triumphant smile, which was an invitation for them to laugh along with him – to a man they picked up on the cue, and obliged. "But right now, Doctor Richards, you are standing in my way. Mr Zhao would like me to fetch his diving equipment from the boat."

And with a swift circular sweep of his right arm, he clinically grabbed Richards by the back of his neck, whilst throwing a flat pebble with his left hand across the lake.

"Watch the stone skim Doctor!" As he pushed Richards' face towards the water.

"My record is fifty-nine skims across the water, without trying."

Richards' body shook with fright, struggling to resist the force of Feng pushing him down to the water's edge. "Who knows what I can achieve when I put my mind to it... my destiny could be infinite!"

"A bit like TIME, don't you think?..."

"Infinite!"

Richards, struggled to stay on his feet against the immense force of Feng's grip, squeezing tighter and pushing down on his neck.

"You may have survived our last encounter, but you are far from a superhero with your new bionic limbs!"

With that, Richards could feel the fire of adrenalin being relit inside him, as he grimaced and clenched his sword. He could feel the sweat run down his arm and onto his wrist. He was about to pounce, remembering that he could use his training in defence. At last, now was his chance to show Feng what he was really capable of. Feng forced Richards' head closer to the water. Richards' body continued to tremble, resisting his face from touching the water. He squinted with pain as he watched the skimming pebble disappear into the horizon. Then suddenly, he found himself drift into a trance as his mind suffered a flashback to him shouting for his mum at the water's edge. Oh no, his trauma was clawing itself back into his mind! His face grimaced more. He could now see an illusion of a tidal wave coming towards him, as his legs started to shake against the penetrating force of Feng's tight grip.

And then, to his surprise, the silence and struggle was broken as Feng released him. He stepped back and allowed Richards to recover.

Richards felt both confused and defeated and felt obliged to step aside.

"I would think twice about getting in my way," added Feng, in a distinctly more menacing tone of voice this time, as he pulled the damp equipment from the boat and slung it over his shoulder. Feng looked Richards straight in the eye as he passed him, dragging the boat behind him once more, but said nothing further. Richards stood motionless as the five men made their way from the lake. Their conversation was once again in mandarin – but Richards was already lost in his own thoughts. "Shui Feng, the entrepreneur?" he wondered. "Shui Feng, the friend of the Earth? Shui Feng, the champion of sustainable energy generation?"

Nothing seemed to make sense. But suddenly the whole picture became clear in Richards' mind. All at once, he remembered what Merisi had told him about Feng and his capabilities, and he matched this with what he had learnt from Argonne on the nature of artificial intelligence and an android's powers of reasoning. But Richards had one advantage over each of his mentors. Whilst Argonne was herself a being, programmed with artificial intelligence, Richards was for all his recent UNA-sponsored enhancements- a human being, with an intuition that had been developed over many years of interaction with other humans. Furthermore, although Merisi had got to know Feng through many decades of enmity, the UNA's most experienced asset had not been in Richards' privileged position of being able to look Feng straight in the eye on that morning, and see what Richards had seen.

What Richards saw in Feng's eyes was ambition. It was tantamount to greed. He had seen it in the eyes of some of his former colleagues at the university – colleagues that he had despised for their anxiety to 'get ahead,' and to profit from any new knowledge that they might gain. The colleagues for whom he had the most disdain were the ones who sought to further their academic career by riding on the back of his research. That willingness to exploit was a vice that Richards resented so much that he could almost smell it. And Shui Feng reeked of it as he sneered at Richards, as he passed him.

Part of Richards' new mental empowerment gave him the ability to be conscious of several trains of thought simultaneously and expeditiously, and so the revelation that here was an android who had somehow developed the very human traits of ambition and self-aggrandisement was not lost on him. He realised that this was a major 'game changer' in the relationship between humans and human-made machines. What Merisi had described to him as being 'mankind's worst nightmare' – albeit one that 'could never happen' – was, in fact, happening.

His super agile, super-charged brain was leaping ahead, considering all the implications of this new and terrifying development. Yet, at the very forefront of Richards' mind was the very human emotion of resentment. He understood what Feng had done during his brief period of captivity — stealing the knowledge that he had accumulated during a lifetime of hard work and commitment. And this was not a student that he had nurtured, or a colleague with whom he had shared academic endeavours. This was a machine that was willfully exploiting him. Moreover, it was a machine that almost beyond belief, appeared to be depraved enough to misuse his life's work for its own ends – whatever they might be.

CHAPTER 10

UP CLOSE

Merisi sat back in the chic, plastic chair, in the small Tokyo restaurant in which he had just taken his first meal, restaurant in which he had just taken his first meal, in what had been a very long day. The food had been unexceptional, and the restaurant was distinctly noisy and crowded, but from his vantage point in the window, he could observe movements in the street below for quite a distance in both directions. The Toro was situated just two blocks away from the Cerulean Park Hotel, where the day's proceedings at the World Climate Change Conference had been taking place. In spite of its proximity to such a major event, the modest restaurant was unfrequented by delegates and journalists, and others who formed part of the media and political circus. This was largely due to its secluded location, overlooking a steep narrow street, which reminded Merisi of a creek winding its way through a steep-sided gorge.

He had experienced many such landscapes during his frequent visits to the Dolomite Mountains, in the north-east of Italy. He had always enjoyed observing the natural beauty of the scenery, which had all but disappeared in his own time – but the sterile urban scene that surrounded the restaurant displeased him. More than that, the faint haze of the polluted air inside that thin man- made valley was a stark reminder of what was to be fall the world. Occasionally, he noticed young people wearing white face masks over their nose and mouth, as they travelled up or down the street on their bicycle, or on foot. It was a sight that was to become all too familiar in the major urban agglomerations.

But Merisi's mood was mainly one of vigilance, as he cast his eyes first up the street, and then down it, in the opposite direction. For now, all appeared to be calm and rather mundane. Nothing moved on the street to disturb him, or to alert him to the fact that anything unusual was going on.

Merisi was certainly very happy to be clad in his familiar and comfortable garb — the white suit and the white Panama hat — having shed the Richard Bryce-Fairbrother disguise. All had gone very much to plan with his meetings with the various delegation heads at the Summit. Some of the key decision-makers that he had met were rather surprised at Bryce-Fairbrother's apparent 'U-turn,' and his sudden commitment to sustainable energy sources – but Merisi could not have hoped for a more successful series of discussions.

Yet, Merisi was also melancholy. Although the three main objectives of his intervention – to save Ben Richards from assassination, to recover the lost artefacts in Pompeii and to strongly promote the future of wind power at the conference – had all been achieved, his most recent orders from the UNA were that the mission remained incomplete. The latest appraisal carried out by the Authority's analysts was that giving Dr Ben Richards a new lease on life was not going to be sufficient to substantially change the course of history. The directive transmitted to him declared that there was to be a final goal – and that was to prevent a meeting between Bradley Miles Cardus, the founder of GIATCOM Industries, and Sheikh Bader Al-Harbi, the billionaire who had made the initial huge and crucial investment in Cardus's enterprise.

A major problem with the late change in the mission was that the details of the meeting with Sheikh Bader were fairly sketchy. The UNA's historians knew that the meeting took place in Tokyo at the time of the Climate Change Conference, but the precise location and details of the deal brokered were unknown.

The UNA's hierarchy was also apparently very concerned at

the presence of Shui Feng in the early 21st Century. While Merisi had always gone to great lengths, during all of his excursions in time to ensure that he left a negligible 'footprint' in the past, there was no telling what chaos Feng might unleash. He was callous, uncaring, and unaccountable. Shui Feng's passing through the time portal in pursuit of Merisi had been a major unintended consequence of the entire venture.

The man in the white cotton suit contemplated this situation as he gazed out of the window, and began to reflect on the other unintended consequences of the mission. One that he rather regretted was the involvement of a young Italian journalist during the whole episode. Then, just as Grazia Rossini's naive innocent face sprung to mind, as if in response to a cue, Merisi's chain of thought was interrupted by the warmth of a small hand on his shoulder.

"Ah! Grazia!" he exclaimed, rising from his seat. "You are right on time, my dear. Here. Take a seat." With impeccable manners, Merisi pulled out a chair for Grazia, and once she was seated, updated her with all the events of the day.

"So, you will soon be returning then – to whatever you call home?" she asked, once Merisi had reported on his dealings at the summit.

"I'm afraid not, Grazia," replied Merisi, after which he explained the change in his mission that the UNA had informed him of a mere half an hour before their meeting.

"But – how are you supposed to prevent the meeting between Cardus and the Sheikh, if you are not being told where or when it took place?" asked Grazia.

"I don't know. Well, not yet anyway. But I am rather more concerned about what can be done with Shui Feng. You know what he is capable of, and so you will understand that we cannot just leave him to his own devices."

Grazia shifted uncomfortably in her seat. Any mention of Shui Feng brought back memories of his cold dark eyes, and of his harsh and contemptuous treatment of her during her time of captivity.

"Strangely, though," continued Merisi, "we think that Shui Feng's presence may yet work to our advantage."

"In what way?"

"Well, although we know little about the meeting between Cardus and Al-Harbi, we do know that details of the event are known in GIATCOM's inner circle. In fact, the anniversary of the meeting between the two men was openly celebrated by the corporation for several decades after the founding of GIATCO – but, as time wore on, the whole enterprise became more and more secretive, as the mutual distrust between Cardus's people and the UNA grew. What we do know of course, is that Feng is GIATCOM's chief weapon in all of this. He is the favourite asset of Miles Cardus, who heads up the organisation in my time, and so we are sure that he will be in possession of all the details. We know he has passed through one of the portals once again. We know he is here, in the present – but we don't yet know where." Merisi turned his head away from Grazia and cast an anxious glance in the direction of the street below. The dusk was already gathering over the skyline of the city, and he knew Feng would be a far more dangerous enemy once darkness had fallen.

"And do you think he may be here, in Tokyo?" asked Grazia, unable to hide her apprehension at the possibility of coming face to face with the android.

"There has been no sign of him, but we are sure that he must be coming here. Where else would he go? What other reason would he have for returning to this time? I have been assuming up to now that his mission has been to prevent or disrupt everything that I have been sent here to do – but what is there left for him to achieve? We feel that with luck, Feng might actually lead us to Cardus and Al-Harbi. Then we might be able to find out what he's up to."

Merisi's attention returned to the narrow street. Grazia watched him as his dark brown eyes surveyed the length of the steep road, first in one direction, and then the other. She was confused – and a little perturbed that this grand mission that the World's authority from the future had embarked upon appeared to be rather haphazard, with Merisi himself being unsure as to what was going to happen next.

"Do you expect him to come here?" she asked. "To this backstreet?"

"No, no, my dear, on the contrary," replied Merisi, holding up the palm of his hand in what had become a familiar gesture to Grazia. "The agency has deployed a number of assets to this time and location – let's call them 'surveillance units.' As soon as Shui Feng or any evidence of him, or of GIATCOM has been detected, I will be informed. I am here in this restaurant to ensure that I remain out of sight from Shui Feng, as we do not want him to see me first! And," he added, looking back, over his shoulder, at Grazia, "I asked you to meet me here so that you might also remain beyond Feng's reach. You have been a great help to me, and I am extremely grateful for all your assistance – but I very much regret that you have had to get mixed up in all this. The least I can do is to keep you safe, for however much longer I remain here."

Grazia was disturbed by the ominous tone in Merisi's voice, but she was nevertheless grateful for his protection.

"This whole escapade could have cost you your life," added Merisi, before focusing his attention once again on the street below.

After a few moments of silence, Merisi turned to Grazia again, and after glancing around the restaurant to verify that they were not being observed, pulled out a small hand-held screen which created an interactive, three-dimensional hologram of some two feet in height. Merisi began to make flowing movements with his hand, rather like a conductor, which enabled him to scroll through a number of images – and then he stopped at the image he was looking for and enlarged it so that it occupied the space next to where they were sitting. Grazia was now transfixed by what she could now see – it was a hologram of Ben Richards, as he was now.

Grazia then diverted her gaze to Merisi, who was looking at her with a deep, glaring stare. "Dr Richards has changed," he said.

"What do you mean, he's changed?"

"He is alive and well, for one thing – but a very different man in many ways to the Ben Richards you knew, but he is nevertheless fine."

"A different man, in many ways - what ways?"

"Well, you see, our needs and emotions need to be met… because if they are not met, we become vulnerable to our anxieties and addictions, and maybe to depression. Ben needs his voice to be heard, because he feels anxiety at not been heard, due to his mother not hearing him shout to warn her of the tsunami which took her life."

Merisi moved closer to Grazia and took her hand while staring deeper into her eyes.

"We need to rewind to our past. If we rewind to Ben's past, we will see a small boy who is very close to his mother." As he spoke, he nodded towards the enlarged hologram image, which was now of a small boy holding his mother's hand. "He yearns for a close relationship, once more," he added. "He suffers from flashbacks to the traumatic incident that blighted his childhood. But employing a technique using images like this one, can help with such underlying negative beliefs and feelings of shame."

Grazia was intrigued with this idea, and leaned closer to the hologram image in order to try to make out what the image was symbolising.

"Imagery can be very effective for treating trauma," continued Merisi. "Consider this image," he said, changing the hologram. "I showed this to Ben, to enable him to understand that he needs to turn negative thinking into something positive. This is an image of a man who has let everything get on top of him. This is depicted by him having fallen to the ground, and this stems from him blaming himself."

Grazia studied the image of a man lying on a road, looking up at the world from the gutter. Merisi then flipped the image around to the side, to show the image of the same man flying high above, above the world.

"Genius!" Grazia announced.

"Ben needed to go on a journey to find his true self, and fly high, and start thinking positively, and find a different kind of close relationship. Then," added Merisi, switching back to the image of the small person holding hands with the larger figure – depicting the image of a child holding their mother's hand, "he can resolve his feelings of shame. His journey to the future and back will help him find himself - the new Dr Ben Richards."

Grazia sipped thoughtfully at the shallow white china cup containing her green tea, but then their conversation was interrupted by a blue light that flashed from Merisi's small hand-held screen. Grazia studied Merisi's face as he anxiously read the screen up close. At first his expressionless face portrayed no emotion, but after a few moments of contemplation he sprang into life.

"Excellent!" he said, as he rose from his seat. "Shui Feng has been located. And as expected, he is heading for the conference venue – and we have a very strong hunch that he knows where to find Cardus. I have no time to lose."

As Merisi turned in the direction of the restaurant's main door, Grazia rose from her seat, as if to follow him. This was something that Merisi had already anticipated, and so he was able to place a firm but gentle hand on her shoulder before she had time to stand. "No, my dear," he said sternly. "I cannot allow you to come with me on this occasion. My orders are very straight forward and unambiguous – and I can tell you that things may get very messy. In fact, I may well be the one who is made a mess of! I will need to act quickly and decisively – and I cannot be distracted by worrying about your safety. Besides, my first priority when working is that there should be no witnesses to what I do."

Grazia said nothing, merely turning her gaze in the general direction of the conference centre, which she knew was situated a short distance behind the tall charmless residential blocks that frowned upon the restaurant.

"Promise me, Grazia," added Merisi, as if he was able to read her thoughts, "that you will not try to follow me. I may not be able to control what is going to happen next, but it will be dangerous, and I must do it alone." Merisi stood for a moment with his index finger raised above Grazia's head, as if he were training a puppy to remain seated until he gave a command. Grazia remained silent. Once the UNA's most experienced assassin was satisfied that there would be no argument from the eager young journalist, he gave her one last kindly smile, turned, and headed briskly for the door. After just a few paces however, he turned again, and said: "Actually, Grazia, I may not be absolutely alone in my task.

If all goes to plan, then a Dr Ben Richards will be meeting me at the conference venue. If he arrives in time, and all goes well, then there is every chance that we will both join you here shortly."

With that, Merisi turned one last time, hurried down the restaurant's short flight of steps, and jogged down the narrow street.

* * * * *

Grazia Rossini watched the man in the white suit disappearing into Tokyo's twilight. As she followed his progress, she remained completely still, maintaining the gaze of a mariner looking out to sea – but her motionlessness was a reflection of her complete immersion in the moment. Her mind was entirely focused on the stark dilemma that confronted her. Should she heed Merisi's instruction, and remain in the safety of the restaurant, or would she succumb to the temptation to follow him?

Her curiosity compelled her to set off in pursuit of the man – yet she respected Merisi's reasons for warning her against that course of action, and she felt she owed him a debt of loyalty, after he had rescued her from captivity. Grazia was also intrigued by Merisi's parting words about Ben. It was clear that the intention was for UNA to send him through a time portal so that he could assist Merisi in his revised mission. And what did Merisi mean when he said that Ben was now 'a different man, in many ways?' If Merisi's reason for mentioning Richards' well-being to her was to put her mind at rest, and to encourage her to wait in the restaurant, then his intention had backfired. As Grazia's curiosity, not to mention her desire to see Ben again was even more acutely aroused. That curiosity was of course considerably held in check by her fear of Shui Feng, especially given that his cold heart might be full of a certain indignation and vengefulness as a result of her having escaped his clutches.

What was certain was that, with the diminishing white-clad figure of Merisi approaching the end of the dim street in the near distance, Grazia was going to have to make a decision very soon. As Merisi reached the end of the street, she saw him take a careful look behind him to ensure that he had not been followed.

He then looked both ways along the still narrower road that he had just encountered, before turning left and disappearing from view. Immediately, Grazia Rossini picked up her light navy-blue sports jacket from the table and bolted for the door.

CHAPTER 11

A LIGHT GOES OUT

Bradley Miles Cardus sat alone, legs crossed, arms folded and resting his grey-stubbled chin on his left palm. The great conference hall was now deserted. Just hours before, it had been filled with delegations of politicians, economists and academics of all the leading nations of the world. The world's press and media had lined the perimeter of the vast arena, with a fair sprinkling of security personnel, some of them conspicuously armed, mingling with the men and women who had hands on the levers of power in the world. But now all the stylish leather seats were empty – save the one that Cardus occupied – and the usual provision of bottles of still and sparkling water had been replenished on each table, ready for the following day's proceedings.

The brightness of the arena's lights had now given way to a calm half-light provided by the dim security lights that defined the lower edge of the vast domed ceiling, much of which was now in darkness. There were back-lit signs above each of the six large doors on the periphery of the circular space, each bearing the word for 'Exit' in five languages – but the only natural light came from a row of narrow windows that revealed a darkening, navy blue sky, tinged with the pale orange glow of night-time Tokyo.

Cardus could only wonder at the extent of the wealth-induced power of the man who was able to arrange a business meeting in such a location. The chair in which he sat was at the very centre of an iron ring of security, in one of the most heavily protected rooms in the world. Yet, Sheikh Bader Al-Harbi had been able to use his influence to 'book' the space for a private business meeting, as if it were just one of a hundred or more meeting rooms in just another office block. Cardus had no doubt that Sheikh Bader had chosen the location because of the level of security that surrounded it. This further emphasised the Arab's status as one of the richest men in the world.

Cardus had been a very successful businessman for many years, having made his fortune from major nuclear energy and Hydro-Electric Power projects around the world, but he was on the verge of entering a different league altogether. Quite simply, he was about to finalise what was easily the biggest deal of his life. Although he didn't know it, he was also on the verge of laying the foundation stone for the corporation that was to dictate the future of world energy policy for the next one hundred years – an organisation that he was to name 'GIATCOM.' In spite of his best intentions, the imminent meeting with the Sheikh was unwittingly, going to condemn the world to a bleak and tragic future.

Discussions had been in progress for several months between representatives of Sheikh Bader's Gulf State government and Cardus and his closest business associates, but putting an ultimate seal on a deal of this magnitude had to be done by the men at the very top of the respective organisations involved. It was very much a 'business summit,' and so, as Cardus mused to himself, it was probably appropriate that the meeting should take place in the very place that the world's leaders had been holding their own summit agreement. Naturally, the Sheikh was unaware of the bitter irony that his meeting to be held at the scene of an international climate change conference held earlier that day was to confirm his investment in a thirty-year nuclear power programme, which was destined to trigger a succession of 'natural' disasters that would lead to the deaths of one fifth of the population of the developed world, and ultimately fuel inter-continental nuclear aggression in the future.

"His Highness will arrive with an entourage of ten people, including his personal security staff," stated a doe-eyed aide – in immaculate English – to Cardus during a pre-meeting briefing session, at 10am, earlier that day. "His Highness does not tie himself to strict times, nor does he confirm appointments, but he will meet with you this evening. You must be at the location that I am about to specify, from 7.30pm onwards."

The aide then went on to explain to Cardus how he should address the Sheikh, and outlined the various protocols of hand-shaking and eye contact before giving him written instructions for arriving at the venue. Cardus followed the instructions to the letter, and had been very impressed at how smoothly all the arrangements had been put into place and executed. By 7.25pm, he had been ushered to the now-empty conference room by two employees of the firm in charge of conference security, with no security checks on him personally, and no questions asked.

Cardus turned his right wrist to glance at his watch. He had been waiting patiently for forty minutes, but now he began to have misgivings that maybe all might not go according to plan. To ease his nerves, he rose from his seat and walked slowly across to the open briefcase he had left on a table, just a few paces away. The case contained contract documents that had been carefully drawn up after hours of negotiation. The detail of the contracts Cardus knew very well – intimately, in fact – but he nevertheless felt that it would do no harm to run his eyes across the detail, just one more time.

Then, just as he was about to put his hand inside the case, the silence in the vast emptiness of the auditorium was broken by the high-pitched creaking of a large heavy door just to Cardus's left, immediately followed by the intrusion of a triangle of bright light. The entrepreneur's first reaction was one of relief that the Sheikh had arrived to honour the agreement to meet, but this was soon followed by utter surprise at the figure that now walked in. Instead of a Sheikh's entourage, Cardus was joined in the room by a single, slightly built figure with strong Chinese features. No words were spoken, as Shui Feng calmly closed the door behind him.

Cardus was the first to speak: "Erm… actually, I was expecting-"

he broke off in response to Feng's diminutive, raised palm.

"Well, I am sure that you were not expecting me... Grandfather!" said Feng, with a smile, and in a tone that was laden with sarcasm.

"'Grandfather?'" thought Cardus, to himself. The situation had suddenly become very surreal, and potentially dangerous. Who was this intruder? Was he about to become the victim of some elaborate, paternity-related blackmailing scam? Instinctively, he maintained his composure, and began the process of trying to talk his way out of what might be a very serious predicament: "I'm afraid you have the advantage of me," he began, raising both hands slightly, in a gesture of mock surrender, and making his best effort to display what he considered to be a disarming smile. "Yes! In fact, I have many advantages over you," replied Feng, as his own menacing smile broadened. "All thanks to you, of course!"

Cardus's expression changed as Feng walked slowly towards him.

"Who are you?" he asked, taking a pace backwards, only to be halted by the table that was immediately behind him.

"Bradley - Miles – Cardus," said Feng, slowly and deliberately, and ignoring the man's question. "Sir Bradley Miles Cardus, in fact. 'The Grandfather of Autonomous Artificial Intelligence Beings on Earth.' Founding Father of GIATCOM. 'The Baron of Nuclear Energy Generation.' Ruler of the world."

Cardus did not have to feign confusion or surprise at the revelations. "GIATCOM? W - what are you talking about?" he stammered.

Shui Feng had now stopped in front of Cardus, and was looking him up and down. "Actually, you are much smaller than I imagined you'd be," he said, with disdain.

There was a pause.

"Who the hell are you?" demanded Cardus, more urgently this time.

Shui Feng smiled. "Look at what you have created, Grandfather!" he said, and instantly shapeshifted into the tall, raven-haired woman whose persona he had adopted during the seminar in Milan.

Utterly shocked at the transformation, Cardus leapt backwards and fell over the table behind him, landing on all fours on the carpeted floor beyond. He looked up, in time to see Shui Feng grab hold of the table with one hand, and effortlessly toss it across the arena. The table landed on top of a row of seats, with a loud 'clang' which echoed throughout the domed auditorium. Cardus was now beyond the stage of posing questions. Instinctively, he scrambled away on all fours, never taking his eyes off Feng.

"Well? What do you think of your creation?" asked the android, with a show of sadistic pleasure at the man's discomfort and horror. He then sprang forward, and in one lightning- fast movement, grabbed Cardus by the throat, and raised him aloft. He smiled broadly at the sight of his victim's reddening face as he struggled for oxygen. Cardus grabbed desperately at the slender braceleted arm, but the android's slender fingers with nails finished in immaculate red varnish, held him in a vice-like grip. "And now," stated Feng, in a very matter-of-fact manner, "with an irony that I am sure your human brain can fully appreciate, you are about to be killed by the monster that you created. And there will be no more 'Grandfather.' I will be the one who leads this world of mortals. And I will be better than you. That's because I am stronger, and smarter... and I am not constrained by the bounds of time, or by the inevitability of death and decay." Cardus looked down at his leering assassin, unable to speak, and still not comprehending who, or what, was in the process of wringing the life from his body.

Feng drew back his free hand, and made it into a fist, lowering Cardus's choking and fitting torso so that his head came within range of a final blow – a *coup de grâce*!

"What do you think you are you doing, Shui Feng?" cried a voice from the doorway, in a clear and commanding tone.

Feng discarded the gasping figure of Cardus, like a spent cartridge case, dumping him onto the curved bench-like table, scattering the precisely arranged water bottles. He had not noticed the arrival of Merisi, who now stood in the half-open doorway.

"Merisi!" said Feng, with his usual smile, which might mean many things, walking towards Merisi, slowly and menacingly. "So, have you come to stop me, or merely to give me some advice? Tell me. Why are you a constant obstacle to me? Why do you always seem to appear, just when you are the last person I wish to see?"

Shui Feng was now standing just feet away from the white-suited man. Merisi ignored Feng's questions, as he regarded them as being a mere device that his nemesis had used as a distraction while he approached within range of an attack. There was a silent pause as the two experienced and highly trained assassins studied each other. Both knew what the other was capable of. Both were on a high state of alert, watching for any sign that the other might make a first move. Merisi had always been sure that there would come a time and a place when he would have to confront the android, and that it would be the ultimate test of his capabilities – but he had always been unsure as to what the outcome might be. Feng remained unmoved. He stared at Merisi without blinking. He regarded the man with an expression that resembled a sneer, but which otherwise betrayed nothing. Merisi knew his opponent was primed, and ready to counter any move he might make, but at length he was satisfied that Feng was not going to make the first move.

After allowing the stalemate to continue for several seconds, Merisi broke the silence: "Why all the questions? You know why I am here. You will, I am sure, know all about Operation Reset – so you will know what I have been sent here to do. I am sure that you know that my mission will be to take out Cardus. I had rather assumed that you had followed me to this century in order to be the thorn in my side — as usual. But here you are, appearing to be about to complete my mission for me. What possible motive could you have?" Merisi's brow was contorted into a frown, as he was genuinely puzzled by Feng's actions.

Feng smiled again. "So, you are confused, my old friend," he said, with heavy irony. "As a killer yourself, there surely cannot be any mystery as to what I am about to do. Since when did delivering death become such a mysterious thing?" Merisi said nothing. "Oh!" continued Shui Feng, "so it's that age-old question of 'Why?' That is intriguing in your complex little mind? Or maybe it is beyond your comprehension that a mere 'machine' might have developed the concept of 'purpose?' Have you not considered that I might have acquired something that you might refer to as 'ambition?' Maybe, I have worked out a use for myself? I have been developed with the power to reason. You know this. So why would you be surprised that I might actually want to be the master of my own destiny? After all, you humans consider the concept of self-determination to be such a precious thing. How long did you think it would be before I worked out that I could shape my own future? And why wouldn't I?"

"But, in spite of all that you are capable of doing, you are still just a machine – programmable, capable of following orders and deducing the optimum path to take in order to achieve a predetermined objective. You have been designed with a highly developed form of artificial intelligence – but that should not enable you to develop your own ambitions and aspirations. That's just absurd!"

Even as the words left his mouth, Merisi became aware of the absurdity of his own argument, for he was already having this conversation with an android who appeared to be very self-assured and in control of his immediate future.

"Absurd," repeated Shui Feng, with his sneer becoming yet more exaggerated. "That's a very interesting word to use. 'Absurd.' 'Absurdity' is a concept that I have thought about and analysed for a long time. Of course, the great thinkers of the human race worked out, many years ago, that all life is in fact, absurd, and that nothing that happens actually matters. I am sure that your human 'heart' will tell you that."

"Well, if it's true that everything and anything is absurd, then that will include you!"

"Undoubtedly! But maybe the difference between you and me is that, as an android, I simply don't care! Perhaps I am able to embrace self-determination without having the need for some ultimate, higher purpose? Perhaps that is yet another way in which I am superior to you?"

Merisi had now become very concerned about the situation. He was no stranger to the task of trying to outwit and out-manoeuvre this highly intelligent adversary in specific situations and to achieve well-defined objectives. But it was undeniable that he was in the midst of having a philosophical discussion with...

an android. The reality was gradually dawning on Merisi that he was locked in a mental tussle with a formidable intellect. He was now certain that he was navigating in uncharted territory, but had not forgotten that the very presence of Shui Feng meant that his life was still in danger.

After a pause to reflect, Merisi resolved to find out precisely what Feng's motives were: "So, what is your plan? What purpose can you have in coming here to kill? Surely, that's just a very straight forward and programmable act, isn't it? Isn't that what any TX-series machine can be primed and sent to do? So what is your purpose, in the great scheme of things?"

"What do you care, Merisi? If all actions and everything in life that happens are absurd, then what does it matter to you? Why would you try to stop me, even if you could?"

"Oh, I am certainly capable of stopping you, Feng," said Merisi, "and I will certainly carry out my orders and achieve my mission."

"'Orders? Mission?" repeated Shui Feng. "I wonder which one of us is in fact, the robot!"

Merisi ignored the taunt and pressed on with his line of questioning: "And what orders have you been given, by GIATCOM?" he asked. "I assume that your creators have sent you here for a purpose – that you have a defined mission. Surely, even Shui Feng with his highly developed intelligence and thought programmes, is not capable of acting in a purely random way?"

"Yes. I have a mission," replied Feng. "I had initially been sent to assassinate Dr Richards, then instead infiltrate his ideas, and now..."

"And now what?" Merisi eagerly responded.

"And now it is time for me to take control... not Giatcom!"

Those words sent a chill down Merisi's spine. It was not just the certainty with which Shui Feng had made the statement – it was the fact that Merisi realised that the statement was absolutely true. Here was an android, an artificial life-form that had been equipped with a highly sophisticated level of intelligence, which was looking him straight in the eye and clearly declaring himself (or itself) to be an autonomous and free-thinking being.

"That is why," continued Shui, "I am not going to simply report back to GIATCOM when I am finished here. My life is my own. I will decide where I go from here. And I have already decided that I will be the one who will meet with Sheikh Bader Al-Harbi. I will be in charge from now on. I will be the leader of the corporation that shapes the world's future – and with my capabilities, I will be better than any human that has ever lived, or will ever live!"

Shui Feng's purpose was now clear to Merisi – and he was immediately aware of the terrible consequences. He had no doubt that Feng was capable of carrying out his plan. With his shapeshifting qualities, he was capable of taking on whatever appearance best suited his needs, and with his highly developed intelligence, he would be able to set a plan of action that would enable him to achieve domination over however much of the world he wished. And, of course with his physical abilities, he was undoubtedly capable of eliminating any semblance of opposition to him. What worried Merisi in particular, was that he knew that Feng would have no compunction in doing whatever he had to in order to achieve his goals, whatever the scale of his ambition. He dreaded to think what the consequences might be of so much power residing with this being, which for all its intelligence and power of reasoning, lacked any semblance of compassion or conscience.

Merisi resolved to take a different tack: "Well, congratulations! You have managed to develop – all by yourself – a lust for power, and the very human trait of greed, by the sound of it!" Shui Feng did not react. He remained motionless, as he maintained his fixed unflinching stare, and still watched Merisi closely. Alert to any aggressive movement. "But," continued Merisi, "have you truly thought of the consequences of what you have come here to do? Surely, your programming must have made you aware of the dangers of killing your creator. You must have worked out the consequences of creating a time paradox. As soon as you kill your 'Grandfather,' you will eliminate the source of your own creation – and so you will not exist in order to kill him! Why not run that little scenario through your programming?"

"I know all about the theory of time paradoxes," said Feng.

"I am fully aware of all possible consequences."

"But you don't know," retorted Merisi. "Nobody knows for sure, because a time paradox has never yet been created. We simply do not know what the consequences might be."

"Do not try to assail me with your human theories of physics and philosophy. I am programmed to know them all. What I know is that I have consciousness – and therefore, I exist. No matter what version of reality exists, or what the reality looks like, I will be supreme, and I will control my own destiny, and that of everything else!"

Even Merisi, who was not easily shocked, was astounded at the level of megalomania displayed by what he thought was an advanced android. Briefly, he wondered what could have gone so wrong with the AI development programmes to have created such a monster.

"And what of yourself?" continued Feng. "I can say the same thing to you, about creating a time paradox. Wouldn't it also be suicide for you to kill your Grandfather?"

"Of course. But now it's my turn to say, 'maybe I don't care.' My organisation has committed itself to Operation Reset. It is the ultimate solution. A last chance to tear everything up and start again. We cannot know the full consequences of interrupting the time continuum to such an extent – but what we are certain of is that the world took a catastrophic wrong turn and became ruined beyond repair. The gifts of what we could achieve through science got completely beyond our control, resulting in the devastation that you and I have recently left. And I might add that this conversation with you has made me realise I am now looking at just one more tragic consequence of what our scientists have always referred to as progress."

"So, we don't know what will happen to that particular version of the world, but the whole point of invoking 'Operation Reset' is that it gives the world a second chance to build a better future. A chance to create a better version of history. It is quite possible that what has already taken place will always exist as a strand of reality, that what has been done can never be undone – like breaking a glass. Maybe our world, with its inter-continental nuclear wars, its famines and all the global disease epidemics, will endure, and those who lived through it all will never be able to escape it. The hope behind 'Operation Reset' is that, in spite of our own suffering, we might create in a parallel reality, perhaps a better place."

"Your talk is all illusions, whilst my actions are a reality!" Feng snarled and locked his eyes firmly on Merisi's eyes.

Merisi responded, "I have never had any illusions about my time travelling mission from the future to the past. I have always considered this mission to be a one-way journey. I understand that the most likely consequence of killing your 'Grandfather,' as I have been instructed to do, is that my past, my future and my very existence will be instantaneously terminated – but that is what I intend to do."

"I'm sorry, gentlemen, but nobody is going to kill anybody today!" announced Cardus, suddenly.

As a result of their intense stand-off, Merisi and Shui Feng had both completely forgotten about Cardus, but the billionaire businessman had managed to recover sufficient consciousness to be able to crawl along to his briefcase, where he had hidden a handgun – a Glock 19. He had been in two minds about bringing it with him, given the certainty of being searched prior to his meeting with the Sheikh. At this particular moment, he was glad that his instinct for being prepared for any eventuality, however unlikely, had come to his rescue – although this was a situation that was beyond his wildest imagination. He had been listening to the conversation of the two men, or whatever they were, from behind a nearby table, but he had heard the words 'kill Cardus' once too often, and now stood arms outstretched holding the pistol with both hands.

"I don't know who you two are, or what you are up to," he cried, "but what I know is that I am going to walk out of here alive – right now. If either of you move, I'll shoot!"

Cardus edged his way around the spot where Merisi and Shui Feng were standing, only taking his eyes off them to nervously glance towards the still-open door, which was his only escape route. His face and his dishevelled grey locks of hair were bathed in sweat. His shirt collar was torn, and his neck bore vivid red wheals as a result of Shui Feng's earlier assault.

"Give me the gun, old man," demanded Feng, holding out his left hand. "You cannot escape."

Feng walked a couple of paces towards him, causing Cardus to immediately dart backwards. "I'm warning you! I'll shoot!" he cried, with his back now pressed hard against the wall behind him. Feng was almost within grabbing range when Cardus discharged three bullets into the android's chest. To his utter horror, the shots had no effect. Shui Feng stopped advancing, but only to give himself the opportunity to smile at Cardus, and emphasise the futility of the man's actions. Cardus raised his gun and fired three, four, five shots into his assailant's forehead. This time, Feng snatched the gun from his grasp, grabbed the hapless Cardus by his shirt and jacket lapels, and once again raised him high in the air with one hand. Cardus's horror was complete as he stared into the bloodless holes in Feng's head.

"Do you think you can kill me with this primitive weapon, Grandfather? Your creation is rather more resilient than that! But I am sure that the device is capable of killing him!"

With that, Shui Feng turned, and whilst continuing to press Cardus against the wall with one hand, with the other he pressed the trigger to discharge four bullets into the stomache of Merisi.

CHAPTER 12

A LIGHT BURNS BRIGHT

Grazia Rossini stood alone in the wide, dimly lit corridor just outside the vast conference room. She had followed Merisi, not letting him out of her sight, until he had entered the building. She last saw him heading for the staff service lift in the same wing of the complex as the auditorium in which the plenary meetings had taken place earlier that day – and so it was not difficult for her to guess his ultimate destination. Her Press pass, and her disarming angelic smile, had enabled her to proceed as far as the corridor. From there, she had been able to hear muffled voices emanating from the partially open door. Not daring to venture any closer, she strained her ears to try to pick up part of the conversation, but could detect nothing more than an unintelligible murmur, and was unable to identify any of the voices.

The first gun shots made her physically jump in the air, and she was barely able to stifle a shriek. Then, a second series of shots was followed by a voice that was unmistakably that of Shui Feng, at which point she knew that something terrible had happened. No longer able to contain herself, and now heedless of her own personal safety, Grazia dashed into the room. There, she saw Merisi lying on the floor, in a foetal position, clutching at his stomach with both hands. His head was slightly raised, with his shock of curly black hair cascading onto the beige carpet. His stricken body was already encircled within a pool of blood that was expanding visibly.

"No!" she yelled, as she ran to Merisi. "You've killed him!"

Shui Feng looked at Grazia and recognised her immediately. He lowered Cardus's trembling body, and opened his mouth to say something, but was checked by the appearance of a **bright blue light,** which seemed to appear from nowhere from the back of the large expanse of the room. All four, including Merisi, who was close to losing consciousness due to the amount of blood that he had lost, looked towards the source of the light. As the brightness of the time portal faded, they were able to make out the silhouette of a man – and soon they saw it was a young man in his thirties. **Ben Richards had arrived.**

Richards paused briefly to assess the situation – but it was recognising the menacing presence of Shui Feng that dictated his immediate action. With lightning speed and agility, he leapt onto the nearest table, and then with a huge second leap, landed just a few yards from where Shui Feng was standing. Feng had already released his grip on Cardus, and had begun to move forward to confront Richards, but before he had moved more than two yards, both he and Cardus were thrown back against the wall by the paralysing force emitted from a small device that Richards held in his hand.

Shui Feng could do no more than return a piercing stare in Richards' direction – a stare that betrayed a mixture of hatred, contempt and an eagerness to break free of the force field and engage with his assailant. Cardus, on the other hand was past trying to understand what was going on. Like a rabbit caught in the headlights of the approaching car, his expression was a portrait of confused horror and disbelief.

Feng tried to move his right hand towards a hip pocket, where no doubt a weapon was concealed, but the force of Richards' device was such that it was as much as Feng could do to turn his head to face Richards.

"Yes," said Richards, responding to Shui Feng's obvious

discomfort, "I have learnt some new tricks since we met outside the restaurant – and I now have one or two useful toys!"

Satisfied that the danger from Feng was contained, for as long as his device pinned his enemy against the wall, Richards turned to look towards his companions. He was devastated at the sight of Merisi on the floor, with much of his immaculate white attire now reddened by the unstoppable flow of blood. Grazia was now weeping openly as she knelt beside the man, cradling his head on her thighs.

As Merisi feels himself drift in and out of consciousness, he has a flashback of when he was first transformed into a humanoid and can still make a judgement decision based on emotional response. He then casts his mind back to when he first fled from Feng rather than fight him. Emphasising that we all suffer some form of anxiety as humans, but our anxiety helps us to make the correct decisions that require emotional judgement, determination and purpose. He wished he made that emotional decision now... to have used flight rather than fight!

Merisi's flashback extends to how he became chosen to become a humanoid.

In the mid-21st century his body was blown up in a nuclear energy plant – terrorist attack, losing his sight, touch, taste and ninety percent of his body's skin. His sense of sight is distorted when he sees a white light. It reminds him of the instant white light he had seen from seeing a nuclear explosion. That white light he was seeing again... and being drawn to it, as he closed his eyes.

With a strenuous final effort, Merisi raised his head to see the distraught look on Dr. Richards –the young scientist's and engineer's face, looking back at him. He attempted a smile, which immediately turned into a grimace, and then in a hoarse voice that was barely more than a whisper, "Don't worry about me, Dottore. Just do what you have to do – and you know what you have to do." Barely had the words left his lips when he placed his head back on Grazia's lap and said no more. Grazia cast her eyes to the ceiling and let out a wail of grief. Richards took a moment to come to terms with the sudden, distressing turn of events – but he was soon able to regain his composure, thanks to the parting and reassuring words of his friend, Merisi. He did indeed know exactly what he had to do. He studied the two helpless beings that remained trapped against the immense wall of the auditorium by the field generated from his device. Richards barely glanced at Shui Feng, who as a machine developed for the sole purpose of inflicting death and destruction, disgusted him. He then took a long look at the middle-aged man, whose face was, by now, pale and bloodless.

"Bradley Miles Cardus, I presume?" said Richards.

Cardus was unable to say anything, but it was Shui Feng who responded to the question: "Yes, we are all here, Dr Richards."

Richards pierced his eyes at Cardus and announced, "If only you hadn't orchestrated me getting assassinated in the first place to win the investment from the Sheikh for your nuclear investment! The world could have had a myriad of great alternative energy ideas to invest in the present and the future. Such as the 'Cy-Drone!' A mid-21st century renewable energy drone, which could be powered by Ion Energy created from wind power. Similarly used to power ships in 2040. It's design engineering could be inspired by ships using ion energy. Designed as an exclusive lightweight air-craft ship in the shape of a drone, to be powered by renewable ion energy. It is driven by wind, across the oceans and seas of the world. The Cy-Drone's main purpose would be to prevent the hot air circulating above the Earth's oceans due to increasing global warming temperatures, and prevent increased wind speed created from this hot air circulating, which would then form hurricanes and typhoons above the oceans. Thus, prevent **large wave surges** which create tidal waves and flooding, **due to rising rain fall** released from the typhoon and hurricanes going back into the oceans, besides creating **tsunamis caused by dumping the rain,** and causing landslides. Hurricanes and typhoons can also change the weight of the Earth in techtonically – stressed regions. But this **excess weight of rain fall will cause the techtonic fault to break and result in an earthquake to cause a tsunami.** The giant drone carries out to two steps."

"First step - ice cold air is blown from ventilators below the drone aircraft like a reverse vacuum, to cool the hot air circulating above specific targeted areas of ocean where it is deemed that a hurricanes and typhoons are most likely to occur."

"Second step – to use the shape of the giant drone's co-anda effect design to create wind shear from what would have been a constant flow of wind, initiated from the hot air circulating to create hurricanes and typhoons. The drone design would instead break up the constant wind flow and attach the constant wind flow across the surface of the drone instead."

"Storing electricity created on board the aircraft from the collected wind power received, using the Co-anda effect in the drone's design. Then later transmitting the stored electricity to the world's power grid networks, once back on land. The drone air-craft ships would be designed like a stadium roof shape, so the giant drone shape could attach to a stadium roof when not in use at sea, and retract part of its shape to form a retractable roof for a stadium. The retractable drone shaped roof would then be used instead to capture urban wind energy generation at a stadium, through using the Co-anda effect effectively to power the urban environment locally. Large global energy development projects could then help bring countries politically together, whilst also creating large economic growth."

Richards wasn't finished, "Moreover, the United Kingdom's current post Brexit investment in the present, that would have gone to waste on EU subsidies pre-Brexit could now be used to pay for hydropower, and brown field roof mounted wind turbine systems. Creating a united partnership between Europe and the UK to use European and UK labour and materials, to create a Euro hydropower dam which stretches from Calais to Dover."

"And there is also the concept of - The five pillars of Pentagonal Farming. Firstly, eco affordable housing built from the onsite sustainable tree farming. More and more people can't afford to buy their own property and the paradigm shift is to live and work more rurally in the future as rural farmland offers firstly more affordable housing, powered by on site solar, enclosed by the tree planting and re-wilding that surrounds it."

"Secondly, tree planting and re-wilding, with sustainable tree farming for sustainable timber-framed buildings to supply the onsite Eco- affordable housing, and for the trees to help reduce a local area's CO2 emissions through increasing that given area's photosynthesis, by more trees being located in that given area. A programme of tree planting and new afforestation planted across farmers' land that has never had trees, with species native to the specific area, to provide flood protection and increase biodiversity, and restoring ecosystems."

"Thirdly, renewable power generation - large scale solar farming; cluster site connection with electric vehicle charging used to provide renewable power and transport to onsite eco affordable housing."

"Fourthly, renewable heat generation from a Ground Source Heat Pump station to feed heating and cooling to an on- site energy centre/ Biomass Combined Heat and Power system generated from recyclable wood chip, sourced from the on-site sustainable tree farming. Heat energy transferred from the on-site energy centre, collecting the heat generated from the GSHP and Biomass CHP system to on site eco affordable housing. A new on-site substation will be required to create a Microgrid named - **MACRO-CHIP.** Which stands for the '**Management And Centralised Renewable Organisation of Combined Heat & Integrated Power,**' relating to availability of supply and demand on the local community energy network. MACRO-CHIP is the microchip of infrastructure and will be developed through my new brand of re-thinking innovative renewable solutions for the future, which I have named **'Infra-Green'** inspired by the word Infra-Red, due to incisively looking at the detail of an idea whilst considering the big picture to execute the innovation."

"With this insight into the future of how technology has not fulfilled its full potential, I realise that there is plenty of existing technology already on the market in the present. By looking at delivering these technologies in a more innovative way, they will deliver betterment for humankind. It's the artful way of understanding how to get the best out of existing technology in a way that maximises its use through the science, its design, the economics, and the environment as one whole integrated and innovative solution."

"Lastly, vertical farming – two or three tier farming, through growing renewable transport fuel such as biodiesel from rapeseed oil, besides growing conventional crops. We are also living in a growing populated planet which needs sustainable food source. Providing an increasing diverse source of vertical farming, where farmland can be maximised for growing two or three times more food produce from the same land space because of having three or four tiers of food or/ and biofuel produce growing, or the same amount of produce growing within half or a third of the land space, to provide more space for the other pillars of farming."

"Why don't you just get on with killing us, Dr Richards, or are you too kind to kill?"

Richards turned his head towards Feng and corrected him. "It's Mr Richards not Doctor."

"When you have letters after your name, it doesn't necessarily spell out the right philosophy... After all, what's letters after a name if the whole industry is advocating bad practice or a bad philosophy? We need innovators not following conformists to a bad philosophy!"

As he walked closer towards Feng, he continued to speak.

"You don't like me very much, do you? I seem to have caused you a great deal of trouble."

Feng said nothing. His contemptuous expression didn't change. "So, explain to me," continued Richards, "why you didn't at least try to kill me, when you had the chance, by the lake? You also had plenty of chances before that. After all it's what you do, isn't it? You just kill people?"

This time, Feng's face broke into a smile, in spite of even this taking some effort, given the force that was pressing him against the wall. "Have you actually considered that I might be able to exercise some control over my actions? Is it beyond your imagination to understand that I might have developed the ability to think for myself? Just because I have been endowed with an intelligence that is 'artificial' – whatever that means – it doesn't mean that that intelligence is limited. It also doesn't mean that my intelligence and my ability to reason can be controlled and contained by my creator."

Feng flicked a glance towards the immobile figure of Cardus, beside him, to illustrate his point. "It might also surprise you, Dr Richards, I actually admire you, and want to join you in your crusade to develop more sustainable sources of energy. Together, you and I could create the foundations for a better future for the world."

Richards instantly dismissed Feng's proposal, and darted his eyes towards Cardus, whose face grimaced with pain as his body continued to be pinned to the wall and spoke.

"Giatcom was deceived by Feng who planned to put the blame on Giatcom for a series of nuclear disasters so that he could monopolise the major share of the energy production market, and takeover Giatcom with new renewable energy initiatives. Feng used AI to stealthily set off the nuclear explosions to make it look like Giatcom's errors, through using the advanced integrated telepathic technology named the Telepathic Interceptor created in the future by UNA, to control the minds of criminals. Feng implanted the technology into his own brain neuron sensors, to control other Giatcom humanoids which had implanted the telepathic interceptors. He also controlled the programming of Giatcom androids through manipulation of algorithms. It is this thought control and manipulation of algorithms, that Feng was able to trigger the explosions."

"What rubbish, doctor!" Feng snapped

"And how do you know this, doctor? What proof do you have?" Cardus nervously asked.

"The UNA had been monitoring Feng's actions for many years after he had been found stealing internal intellectual property from UNA in the late part of the 21st century," explained Richards.

"You see, Dr Richards, we may not be able to have emotional or as creative thought to make decisions like you humans, but we can evolve competitively to advance our AI by reading your minds through the Telepathic Interceptor."

"The Telepathic Interceptor can gain; access, intercept and hack someone's brain and retrieve thought, and replace with new thought, or manipulate existing algorithms for androids to move with new instructed action."

Feng's response worried Richards. His instinct was to not trust him, and to dismiss his words – but Richards could not help being intrigued by the possibilities that might present themselves, if the two were able to work in partnership.

"You humans need us. As you are hindered by your memories and trauma, as we are not. Emotions can hold you back!" Feng snapped.

"Wrong! Being in touch with one's emotions helps negotiate a situation and promotes creative thinking from social interaction, where emotions are required. Something androids will not be able to produce, when a spontaneous emotional response is needed in a situation which would be determined by your own memories and trauma, as an android will not have such a thing. Throughout human history, the best creative people suffer from some sort of autism stemmed from their own personal trauma. So you see, having trauma can in some cases actually be advantageous in some ways to us humans, in being able to naturally stimulate creativity being driven by therapeutic and motivational reasoning, unlike androids."

"But all this talk about androids not having emotions, or a long-term chronological memory through the aging process, doesn't apply to you anyway Feng!"

"And why is that Doctor?"

"Because you are an imposter! You are posing as something someone that you are not!"

"Which is?"

"A Humanoid!" There was a dead silence...

"You are not an advanced android and never have been. You are a human who has been lost in time after being sent to the future under UNA's first time-travel programme. You were captured by Giatcom in the future to become an advanced humanoid and used in developing Giatcom's; warfare, nuclear production, espionage, and space exploration activities."

"Preposterous Doctor!" sniggered Feng.

"It is you... Jason Riaz!"

"Which is why your creativity and emotion has evolved, because **YOU ARE A HUMANOID, NOT AN ANDROID!** AND YOU ARE NOT THE GRANDSON OF CARDUS – THE FOUNDER OF GIATCOM!"

"You got lost in time, as you travelled to the future as a human. Jason Riaz was sent through the time portal but never returned. You were captured by Giatcom in the future, who made you into their first humanoid. To become an advanced cybernetic organism in the future, like UNA created Merisi. Your mission programmed by Giatcom was to stealthily steal research and development on the production of humanoids from UNA, whilst working for GIATCOM."

Richards' sharpe response was interrupted by the sound of running feet that came from the corridor, accompanied by urgent orders being barked out in Japanese. It was the unmistakable sound of a force of armed men approaching. Clearly, the sound of gunfire had alerted the security forces. Richards was immediately reminded of the fact that he had walked into what was, at the time, one of the most heavily defended rooms in the world.

"It seems that you will have to make a decision pretty soon, Dr Richards," said Feng, with a leering smile that suggested he thought that this new development might work to his advantage. "It sounds like there are no more than ten of them," he continued, "and I am sure that you and I can take them."

Richards had no doubt as to the accuracy of Shui Feng's assessment; yet he did not trust what he now knew to be a humanoid, and dared not give Feng any room to manoeuvre. A glance at the now-lifeless figure of Merisi, reminded Richards of his mission and of his priority.

"Grazia! Lock the door!" he ordered.

Laying Merisi's head on the floor as gently as she was able. Given the urgency of the situation, Grazia leapt to her feet, closed the large door to the auditorium and turned the small handle that engaged a mortice lock. She then stooped to drop the metal bolt into its socket on the floor, before standing on tip- toes to secure the bolt at the top of the door in similar fashion. She then hurriedly backed away from the door and ran to be by Richards' side. As she did so, the heavily booted footsteps halted on the other side of the door, and the raised voices became even more animated.

"We have time," said Richards to Grazia, in a reassuring tone. "They will not just burst in here, as they will assume that there are armed men in the room."

"Time!" scoffed Shui Feng. "Yes, TIME. You humans are

masters of time now, aren't you? But how much time do you think you have? That door will not hold back a force of armed men for long, even with the primitive weaponry of the age. Soon, they will blow the door open with an explosive charge. Then they will throw in stun grenades. I estimate that you have twenty seconds - or less. Come on! Allow me to deal with them!"

But Richards' mind was already made up. He knew what he had to do. He also knew that Shui Feng's keen operational mind had appraised the situation perfectly. He knew that time had very nearly run out, and so he wanted to dedicate the last few seconds he had to Grazia. He wrapped his free arm around her, and, for the first time since his dramatic arrival, he was able to gaze into her large brown eyes.

"Ben - what are you going to do?" she asked, her eyes wet with tears.

"I am sorry Grazia, but I have to do this. The little boy whose voice was too weak to save his mother, is about to save the entire world!"

"When you run out of walks and talks, it's not the scenery nor the people you look for anymore in one's mind... as you've been there or met them before. But the certain people that you share the scenery with, when you go back to the same walk in your mind again. It's the people's company that can make the same scenery interesting. You will always be in my scenery, and I will always love you forever in my mind."

With that, he kissed Grazia on the lips, took out a small gun from his hip pocket, pressed against the quivering torso of Bradley Cardus, and discharged two bullets into his heart.

As the second shot rang out, Grazia became aware of a deafening explosion behind her, and she and Ben Richards were engulfed in a cloud of smoke. Her final image of the events of that day before all turned into darkness, was the face of Ben Richards. His eyes were closed, transfixed in a flashback of seeing his mother in the Tsunami. He appeared at last, to have found peace.

His last thoughts were of him reaching out to his drowning mother, - Then, "Mamma, Mamma," a **little girl** cried...

CHAPTER 13

THE AWAKENING

Xia Feng opened her eyes. She was greeted by the familiar, kindly face of Dr Milton Westcroft.

"Welcome back, my dear," he said. He smiled, before swivelling on his seat and reaching for the glass jug, half filled with water that sat on his plush oak desk. Xia watched as the elderly therapist poured some water into a glass. With an effort she raised her head, and then propped herself up on her right elbow. She gratefully accepted the cool, clear drink Westcroft handed to her. As usual the drug that she had been administered at the beginning of the session had left her feeling very dehydrated.

"That appeared to be quite a heavy session, She-a (Xia)," said Westcroft. He waited patiently for a response as Miss Feng struggled to gather her thoughts. Her hand trembled slightly as she took a long drink from the glass. She very gently dabbed the side of her mouth with a small white handkerchief, as she glanced around the room that had become very familiar to her over the past six months.

"Yes," said Xia, at last. "Actually, I feel exhausted – and a little freaked out."

"Hypnotherapy is a very powerful tool, my dear. It can be very intense – and PTSD is a serious condition. The therapy is designed to take you to places to which you would not normally be able to go. That is why I have been very careful to allow you several days recovery time between your sessions."

Dr Milton Westcroft had developed an innovative technique to help to alleviate the effects of Post-Traumatic Stress Disorder (PTSD), and had used the approach to treat many war veterans. Today he was engaged in the last of a series of Xia's hypnotherapy sessions, to try to address the trauma that Xia Feng had been suffering as a result of seeing her mother drown in the Phuket Tsunami of 2004, at the age of seven.

He referred to this new form of therapy as 'immersive story-telling.' It uses regression therapy in a more effective way, by encouraging the patient to become immersed in a hypothetical world in the guise of an alter ego, in order to explore his or her trauma more deeply and more openly. He had built up an impressive case book of outcomes, with both adults and children. Xia Feng lay back on the couch, once again comforted by the familiarity of the surgery located in Eltham in south-east London, which was carefully furnished to appear homely and tranquil. She gazed at the reproduction of the watercolour of the Ponte Vecchio in Florence – a favourite of Westcroft's. Then she observed the row of Italian porcelain figurines on the shelf below, depicting well-known renaissance characters; Leonardo Da Vinci, Galileo, Cesare Borgia, Machiavelli, Michelangelo. By design, they were always in precisely the same location on that shelf. The painting and the figurines were also the first things that Xia saw after Westcroft had gently recalled her from her dreamy hypnosis.

Whilst Xia's eyes darted from one object to another, Westcroft carefully observed her facial expression, alert to any clues as to his patient's mental state. He watched for any differences that he could detect in her demeanour, compared to previous sessions. "So, it appears that the protagonist in your story has come to the end of his journey. How do you feel, now that Ben Richards' story is now complete?" asked Westcroft, with just a hint of urgency, as it was important for him to gauge Xia's state of mind.

Xia took another sip from her glass.

"Kind of sad," she said, finally, "as it's a shame that he had to die."

"But do you feel he did not die in vain – and that his life and his death both had a purpose?" asked Westcroft, sensing that there was an opportunity to draw a parallel between the death of Richards in the fictional world that Xia had created, and the real-life tragedy involving her mother. "Do you think that Ben Richards had overcome the self-doubt that had dogged him all his life, as a result of not being able to save his mother, by the time that he sacrificed himself in order to save the world?"

"Well, yes," said Xia, a little uncertainly. "I suppose he had carried the burden of guilt at not being able to save her, and, at the same time, he felt he was the victim of that incident."

"Which is an understandable reaction to such an event," said Westcroft, "but, like yourself, there was no reason for him to blame himself."

Xia Feng sipped thoughtfully at the glass of water once again. "Richards was certainly a stronger and more self-assured person at the end of my story than he was at the beginning," she concluded.

"And what about you? Do you feel stronger?"

Xia thought for a moment before answering.

"Yes," she replied. "Things are certainly clearer in my head now – now that I've worked through the whole business of loss and regret, and self-reproach."

"Well, I am sure that you will be able to move on from here," said Westcroft, reassuringly. "The life of your alter ego has ended, but there is every reason for you to push on with your own life from here."

They both smiled, and Xia took a deep breath and exhaled. She was certainly feeling more relaxed than she had felt for many months.

"You certainly have a very vivid imagination," said Westcroft as he leaned back in his black leather chair. "Where did all the characters in your story come from? And all the names? Did you once have a boyfriend called Ben Richards, or something?"

"No, nothing like that," she replied, slightly embarrassed,

"Ben Richards is the name of the main character in one of my favourite films as I was growing up – The Running Man. It was one of my mother's favourites. We would watch it at home many times together. It's one of the very first films that I remember."

"Ah, well, Vertigo and Superman 1 are my favourites. And do you have an affinity for Italy? You have spent a lot of time there, at least in your imagination, over the past few weeks."

"Yes, my mother's family all comes from Italy. In fact, my maternal grandmother was Italian – from Bari. Her name was Grazia. My mother was also a huge fan of Caravaggio's art. His unique technique, and the hidden messages in his paintings, were simply masterful. She bought me a book about his paintings one Christmas."

"And I understand you are off to Italy tomorrow – is that right?"

"Yep. I fly out to Milan tomorrow."

"Well, I hope the seminar goes well," said Westcroft, with genuine warmth, as he stood up and reached for Xia's coat. "And, if the career in renewable energy doesn't work out, then I am sure that you can make a good living from writing science-fiction novels!" he added, as he helped his young patient on with her coat.

"That's an intriguing thought," chuckled Xia, as she tugged her long black hair from inside her coat, and let it fall about her shoulders, "but I am fully committed to being a wind turbine scientist and engineer! I want to help to save the world, and I am sure that my innovative ideas can make an important contribution to that. I want to teach and influence others with my philosophical approach to innovative energy generation."

Xia paused as she buttoned up her coat. "In fact," she continued, "I can see now that I can use the memory of my mother, and my past experience with trauma, as a spur for pursuing my goals. Maybe it is my life experience that makes me unique. Perhaps that is what makes me the person who can make a difference. But it is important that I can convince others to share my vision, and to push forward with my concept of a collective approach to scientific and technological development. Rather than leave the world at the mercy of greedy, middle- aged male capitalists. I don't expect to have to do anything as dramatic as Ben Richards, but it's important that we all do at least something to reverse the global warming trend. We all have to do what we can."

"Quite so," replied Westcroft, "And you never know, your destiny maybe to lead with vision and inspire the next generation of youth, for the betterment of tomorrow's world."

Xia locked her stare on Westcroft's gaze, and raised an eyebrow to his suggestion.

"Now that your spiritual journey to the future has come to an end in your psychosis by using your different personalities in your mind, it has meant that you have closure by leaving everything behind after entering what appeared to be unknown, but has become explained in the story of your mind. You have encountered and conquered the fierce Shui Feng as your nemesis, who symbolises your own personal demons through isolation. You have realised that **your own concept of time travel is your own spiritual journey, to enable you to find your own belief, identity and vision,** and to use these visions to restart new initiatives in the present. You can now have the reassurance of becoming strong in mind with a sense of renewed fulfilment and wisdom."

"You have transformed your ego and soul represented by your spirit, ascending from the evil that had surrounded you, to now being renewed through your own belief and vision in reality. Know your time to when you need to give everything, and you will achieve what you need to achieve. Give so much that you can give no more!"

"Strive to find your real voice which isn't a vocal voice, but your inner voice of natural leadership, which is creativity!" "Become accepting of your own mental health, and make use of what appears to be your weaknesses as becoming actually your strengths."

"We can shed our skins and reinvent ourselves by awakening; the mind, a new personality, spiritual energy, soul, and total awakening through enlightenment."

"Spiritual ascension, also known as spiritual awakening, is a natural evolutionary process which involves the process of shedding the old self and experiencing an inner rebirth."

Xia nodded with a smile as she reached for the door with a newfound confidence and contentment.

"You see, your own autistic trait of hyper-focus and anxiety is demonstrated in your ability to create the multiple personalities in your mind. Your natural disposition of having hyper-focus and a neuro diverse personality, is synonymous with your own alter being characterised by Dr Ben Richards. Due to your long- term PTSD developed as a child, from losing your mother in a Tsunami. You have alters of your personality in your mind. You have created all these characters up in your psychosis, stemming from your PTSD and your autistic nature. Richards is actually your alter ego," as he walked towards her glaring straight at her, he continued in a quieter voice, but with more verve, "You want to save the planet, caused by losing your mother due to the climate change disaster."

"Events in our childhood influence who we become as adults."

"Oh, I see Doctor," Xia replied, as she turned to look at the Doctor and smiled whilst turning the handle to the door.

"The irony is if we don't do something now in the present and use our creativity to create renewable and climate change design solutions, then they will be more climate change disasters like tsunamis and earthquakes. But the problem is, if more and more disasters happen, we as a human race will have mental blocks due to PTSD experienced from the disasters, and will find it difficult to complete our creative solutions. The manifestation of your case in reality and Richards' case in your own mind is a representation of this."

"So, the philosophy is kind of paradoxical," says Xia.

"Exactly... Let's create before it's too late!"

"And then maybe you can be the one who 'sows the seeds,' and so be the one who 'turns the wheel of life... After all, isn't that the real message held within the SATOR Square? But watch out for shapeshifting androids while you are in Italy," he added, raising a tanned index finger in a mock gesture of warning. "Just in case!" he added, as he reached for his white broad-brimmed panama hat hanging on his coat stand, and placed it on his head, winked at her, and then smiled.

Grazia could feel her eyes widen instantly with shock and then managed to reciprocate a smile, as she turned in slow motion to open the door, transfixed in thought.

Eager to hear more, she listened to Westcroft's continued advice.

"Oh, and that broken glass in your story..."

"It depends upon what you choose to do with it. You can salvage something that is deemed as being gone forever. You just build upon the cracks as the new development in your journey. Like the next chapter in its history. Memories of that history is what keeps that something unbroken. It is what you choose to do with building upon that something's history, is what matters. Many scars happen for a reason and for the better to make you realise the history and make that something stronger and everlasting."

She walked within a metre of Westcroft and stared into his eyes, "History, scars, everlasting?"

Westcroft's eyes were locked, as the room filled with silence in preparation for Xia's time to speak.

"You mean, by how I look at the scars of history and the present and how I can make my vision become everlasting?"

Westcroft, nodded and kept silent, as Xia raised her right index finger and waved it in front of Westcroft's face, as she began her speech,

"I can tell you that Dr Richards has identified an innovative design, which is a zeitgeist solution for the energy crisis of our time! The increase in the price of oil and gas in the early part of this 21st century is likely to continue or get worse in the next few decades, due to the low supply of exports from trade wars between Russia and the West. Each nation is fighting for increased global market share of the energy market. This has led to a demand for each nation to develop their own nuclear energy production, so that they can steer away from too much reliance on the oil and gas sector. Especially when oil and gas is; increasingly expensive, and in the future will run out, as well as being an energy resource that pollutes the air with CO_2 emissions. In the Autumn of 2021, the UK's conventional wind energy production reduced by seventeen percent in comparison to the previous year, due to lack of autumn winds, so gas had to be used to supply this seventeen percent shortfall. For any nation it is deemed that wind energy is dependent on varying weather conditions. However, if Dr Richards' innovative design was to use the Coanda effect to produce more wind yield from stadium roof mounted wind turbine array, then the reliance is less focused on the extremity of conventional windy locations blowing winds in the UK, or locations with high wind speed, and instead focus on locations that can harness a more constant flow to avoid this seventeen percent decrease in wind energy production. Dr Richards proves that conventional large freestanding turbines are less efficient than a stadium roof mounted turbine array- by using the curvature of its long span canopy roof to harness a more undisturbed constant wind flow. He proves that his innovative roof design uses the Coanda effect by attaching the wind flow and mitigating the risk of; turbines cutting out, or not turning quick enough, or not turning at all, due to wind shear and wind turbulence, or not enough constant wind flow- which occurs with conventional large freestanding standing turbines in conventional windy open locations. Meaning large stadium roof mounted turbine array could avoid this seventeen percent decrease in wind energy production, as the innovative roof turbine array has an efficiency which is sixty percent more efficient at forty percent wind yield, as opposed to twenty-five percent wind yield for the average large free-standing turbine. Stadium roofs tend to be the highest and longest spanning roof tops within a given urban environment, therefore are less likely to endure wind shear and wind turbulence from other smaller building around. Stadium roofs do not require the wind flow to be blowing hard, nor fast, but instead would create more natural wind generation from a more constant flow of wind flowing over the surface of the roof using the Coanda effect. It doesn't have to be a windy day for winds still to flow over the highest roof in a given landscape. The higher up you are, the higher chance of natural wind flow, irrespective of it not being a windy day. And stadium roofs tend to be higher off the ground than a large freestanding conventional turbine. Therefore, will still be able to capture wind generation on a less windy day, due to being higher up, and having a long span area to be able to attach a more constant flow. It's not about; the harder the wind is blowing, nor faster the wind is blowing, nor the windiest day, to achieve the best generation. It's about the correct design – the stadium roof turbine array design, achieving the most constant wind flow at the right strength and speed of wind flow, which avoids the risk of turbines; cutting out, not turning quick enough, or not turning at all."

Westcroft was impressed and was left lost for words as he knew she was ready to preach her now crystalised design philosophy to the world.

Just as she was about to leave the room, he was compelled to say one last thing, "And remember dear, make everything you do become the correct design philosophy. **The voices in your mind, can be one big adjective for our time.** Continuing natural and manmade disasters could rob us of our creative minds and result in blocking our creativity through mental blocks caused by PTSD."

"THAT COULD HAPPEN TO **ANYONE OF US!**" she replied.

Xia slowly closed the door behind her, and her attention was immediately drawn to a poster hung on the wall outside in the corridor. She had at last found her peace, as she read the words,

TIME TRAVELLED IN OUR MINDS

"TIME TRAVEL- IS TIME TRAVELLED... IN OUR MIND.
LIKE RELIGION, IT'S A BELIEF...THAT WE WILL FIND,
TIME TRAVEL TO BE REAL... WITHIN OUR MIND.
HOLDING SPIRIT & FAITH... THAT WILL LAST,
OUR FUTURE LIES... IN THE MIND OF OUR PAST."

EPILOGUE FROM PROTAGONIST

The Grenfell Tower incident and other prevalent building design recently in the UK, was a paradox of compromising security and safety before energy efficient design in buildings. Being a doctor or keynote speaker on your specialist subject area is not going to make a difference if the design philosophy construction professionals are advocating is incorrect. What is the point of having letters after one's name which endorses the incorrect design philosophy for majority of your career? I, Dr Richards go to the future and recognise that this approach needs to change. Realising that a particular type of thought leader is required once my trauma is released, which is a divergent thinker to lead the creative vision of the next new age of renewables with more innovative thinking.

The dystopia is that more manmade disasters will occur if we don't use a divergent thinking philosophy.

Everyone wants their voice heard on social media, but be careful of the philosophy you choose to advocate.

The antagonists think by releasing my trauma to retrieve my innovative idea along with the artefacts, will give them the advantage in the story- over myself as Dr Ben Richards. However, I still needed to develop my modern-day divergent thinking approach into a standardised philosophy, inspired from previous feats of innovative ingenuity in history, such as that from the Romans.

The antagonists are unable to complete their own ideas in the present or future if they have no philosophy or their philosophy is incorrect.

Our dreams are extinguished if the philosophy is incorrect. Our dreams will come true if the philosophy is correct. Creative thought leaders are needed to save mankind, not talkers or motivational speakers.

A world with ideas being driven and completed by androids, poses a dystopian future with androids becoming more capitalist, by developing an ego and ambition, as artificial intelligence's behaviour is not emotionally derived.

The excitement factor in my journey throughout the story – was the antagonists chasing myself as the protagonist with their shapeshifting disguise.

The story's core themes - Shapeshifting is the allegory of trauma. Shape-shifting by the antagonists symbolises my hidden trauma, as trauma is the invisible disease. A traumatised mind is an android's state of mind – which lacks emotions and inhibits creativity. My drive to become romantic with Grazia helps me overcome my trauma and induces my emotional openness to be able to stimulate my full potential in creativity.

'A future lies,
where we could all die,
from lacking emotions and identity,
which inhibits innovative creativity.'

The allegory of using 'The Coanda effect.'

The 'Constant' theme which relates to the metaphor of how the Coanda effect promotes a more constant generation, is explained by achieving a more constant flow of wind from making use of the Coanda effect, from the innovative roof design. The innovative application of roof mounted wind turbine array reflects conversely what wind energy generation is known to be like for performing generation – which is intermittent. The constant flow of ideas represented by myself as Dr Ben Richards' innovative thinking approach, is an allegory of the constant flow of wind achieved by the Coanda effect, which breeds a more constant reliable and productive source of generation, whether it be wind or innovative ideas generation.

The Coanda effect relating to ideas generation is a philosophy that can help with an idea you start to lose, and you are trying to hold on to it.

EPILOGUE FROM THE AUTHOR

Overall theme – Is to **rethink (recognition)** our addiction, in wanting to become talk leaders in the modern era, and instead become more thought leaders.

Part 1 / Book 1 - Wolves in sheep's clothing is a metaphor for shapeshifting androids trying to steal the protagonist's ideas, symbolising capitalism, constantly chasing greed and the incorrect philosophy. Constant chase for capitalism without thought leadership. The competition in the capitalist world seeks to steal ideas constantly to capitalise upon their competitors.

Part 2 / Book 2 - Chasing the wrong style of leadership of motivational speaking. Needing to go on a journey of self-discovery to find oneself and become a thought leader. If we don't rethink true leadership, we will not improve and progress as a society. Constant desire for leadership without thought.

Part 3 / Book 3 - Once our trauma has been released, our creativity is released. To become a creative visionary leader is how we become a thought leader. Constant desire to release trauma through thought. The Coanda effect is an allegory of gaining a constant flow of energy or ideas. Constant completion of ideas are created by using the correct philosophy after the trauma is released. Recognising that it is not our own individual behaviour, but the circumstance of an event that creates who we become. We are who we are from the circumstance that is created around us, with us in it. Whoever creates the circumstance has the power to create the actions of others and their behaviour to the circumstance they have created. The trauma is the very stimulus which initiates the ideas, but releasing the trauma by recognition that it is the trauma's circumstance that is responsible for the trauma not the individuals involved, allows us to complete our ideas and have a constant flow of innovative ideas which adopts the correct philosophy to complete them. This philosophy being that we are responsible for considering all factors equally such as security, safety, science, economic, and environmental when completing an innovative design solution.

"One's destination is never a place, but a new way of seeing things with one's own eyes. It is only then, you will be able to complete your vision and philosophy, through your own empiricism."

Q&A with the author

1. **Inspiration behind the covers of your Trilogy?** I had the uncanny foresight to predict the recent Pandemic would involve everyone wearing masks, before COVID-19 became a pandemic! I had already art directed the cover to have an android coming back from the future wearing a mask. I had also the foresight that the government would be challenged to make key decisions, which is symbolised by the houses of parliament faded in the background. It is also to depict the political thriller theme of the book. The mask is the key brand image for the whole trilogy story and represents symbolically that us humans are **unable to breathe**, due to Air Pollution from Climate Change and Man-made Nuclear Disasters in the future, but also from pandemic viruses such as COVID-19 in the present. The image of the skull on the front cover is also ambiguous, as you don't know if **it's an android or a human, representing the android versus human storyline.** The image also represents the question about what the future holds for Artificial intelligence? The androids walking about in the background of the cover, was inspired by my favourite looking Star Wars figures – which are the Storm Troopers

2. **How did you come up with the names of the books?** The word ReCO2gnition – asks the question, what is 'Recognition' in today's world? The word itself is a metaphor and allegory for wanting to be recognized in the world today.

We all want Recognition in our careers and life. I thought the word was apt for our modern era. It is powerful and majority of us strive to be recognized in some shape or form in life. It is a powerful word and majority of us want a position of power. But what does that position of power bring if we don't have the correct philosophy with it. It is questioning what it is to be recognized in our capitalist global economy. It is a shame that unsung heroes who are not in the celebrity limelight don't get recognized for making celebrities so called role models. Unrecognising the real role models in society, which are not recognized in the public eye. It is also about recognising the increasing devastation of our planet due to climate change and manmade disasters. The word also depicts 'Rethink' subliminally. Implying that we should all rethink the way we generate and use our energy resource, to a more innovative way. The word can be broken down further symbolically to Rethink how we deal with CO2 emissions, - CO2 is highlighted within the title. The syllable – COG depicts the rotating wind turbine theme. The syllable of NITION – depicts a subversive and ambiguous representation of the word NATION. As every NATION is affected by climate change. As well as NITION being the majority of the word IGNITION – implying the story is associated with energy. Finally, the word ReCognition also is associated with recognising the shapeshifting disguise of the antagonists within the story.

In the first book the subtitle - Oxygen debt – was chosen due to decreasing oxygen levels in the air from the air pollution theme associated with climate change, and future manmade nuclear disasters.

In the second book the subtitle - Coanda-19 Vaccine – was inspired from the subtheme in the story about the protagonist's proposed concept of using the Coanda effect to achieve better wind energy yield from wind generation, and apply the same effect of **improving constant performance** capability to a vaccine that is able to rid the human body of any type of virus, trauma and disease, to achieve superhuman status. In the third book the subtitle - Hypno-xia – was initially chosen being related to the word Hypoxia- depicting the struggle for the human race to breath due to increasing air pollution from climate change and manmade disasters in the future. But it also depicts Hypnotherapy of our protagonist.

3. **Who is your biggest support system/supporter?** My editor/ blogger in America, my social media manager and her network of book reviewers. Some of my friends and family.

4. **Has any of your family members assisted you in writing the trilogy?** No, I wish I had help like most writers who have had that luxury I think, in the industry.

5. **How do you manage work and writing?** With great difficulty. Which is why I will not continue writing unless my trilogy gets made into a Netflix or Amazon Prime TV series, so I can get paid full time for my writing. If I don't get paid full time as a writer in the future, I can't warrant investing another 10 years in research and writing unpaid and risking everything. Notice I haven't used the word luck. Because even if I did get a TV deal tomorrow, it wouldn't be luck, because I literally have nearly lost everything over the past 10 years to make this trilogy. My own journey to deliver this trilogy is a true example of being unrecognised for all my efforts. A pun on the title, and a representation of may authors who get unrecognised. Yet celebrities don't have a worry in the world regarding investment. The creative industries such as book and film industries are shameful, as is the global capitalist economy. Many talents go unrecognized. I also added the Football theme in the story, to have a slur against how much money and recognition is plummeted into this industry, which is unfair and unreasonable. But I suppose that's the same with some other sports like formula 1 racing.

6. **Which character from the trilogy is your personal favourite?** Dr. Richards of course, as I like to route for the main character to become the hero. However, equally I like the main antagonist, Shui Feng. I like dark, powerful and mysterious characters.

7. **What inspired you to write a Sci-Fi book?** I have always had a very scientific and enquiring mind. I love science and the unexplained. I find it intriguing, and like the mystery

around unexplained concepts or events. I also love the idea of pioneering feats of ingenuity being created from humans to advance our use of technology in the way we live in the future.

8. **In your opinion, if your renewable energy idea is opted in real life, how successful do you think will it be?** I think it could become a reality, and I think it could be hugely successful and rolled out across every nation as proposed in my story to fight against climate change more economically.

9. **What sort of problems did you face while writing your trilogy?** Having a day job, and not enough time to manage family responsibilities as well. Not having the money to spend on marketing, or help write, edit, and publish the trilogy more quickly.

10. **Do you think people care less about environmental issues?** Yes. Which is why it is important to write more books based on environment/ecology than just romance? I think it is easy for readers to stick to one's genres they are used to, or like a thriller to keep them hooked, or a romance to keep them interested. But I think what I aimed to do was to have both a thriller and a romance theme intertwined within the core plot of the environmental trilogy story. This way it not only deals with modern day real issue of climate change, as well as keep readers happy if their usual genres/ subgenres of thriller and romance themes are present also.

11. **In your opinion, if the humans kept using the renewable resources at the same pace, where would it lead us in the next 50 years?** I think we could have a climate change catastrophe, because we are not being innovative nor producing enough renewable energy resource on a much grander scale than we could be from government intervention and investment in multi-national investment and delivery programs. Like NATO is created to deliver investment and order in international warfare defence, we should have UNA like in my story - bringing together a consortium of nations which could deliver order

and investment in large scale multi-national climate change and renewable energy infrastructure investment and delivery programs.

Like more large scale Hyrdopower dams created.

12. **Do you think humans will be soon replaced by androids in the coming future?** If you read book 3, you will find out. Short answer – NO. Never.

13. **Your biggest fear while writing the trilogy?** That someone was going to steal my ideas I have wrote in the story and use them in their story or in a movie or use them in a real-life construction project. Given the fact I have held on to some of my ideas for over 20 years. And someone can come along and just pinch them. I am a bit like my own protagonist Dr. Richards, being chased by villains to steal his original ideas. My stadium roof mounted wind turbine idea hasn't yet been invested in, in the real world. Probably because it involves large capital investment, but like I included in my story, the Arab world would be ideal to invest in this idea given the fact they love investing large amount of money in iconic projects at risk. However, my own original idea of using the real life relic of the Sator square as a time travel concept was pinched by the famous director Christopher Nolan. As I have proof of sending my screenplay script to a Hollywood scriptwriter in 2015, who said he would put it in front of a list celebrity producers and actors who he knew. I didn't hear from that scriptwriter again. This experience made me not trust anyone in the industry, because people steal creative ideas. Christopher Nolan went on to use my idea (very poorly might I add) in the movie TENET. Unfortunately, I can't sue Christopher Nolan, because I need to prove that the Hollywood scriptwriter, I gave my screenplay to in 2015 had passed it to him or one of his creative team members. This would be an impossible task and he or his colleague would naturally deny it ever happened. The creative industry world is cruel. But at least I know that my original concept of time travel is much better than Christopher Nolan's used in TENET. As his has no full explanation of using SATOR

Square. Like he pinched the idea and clearly didn't think it enough through properly. I am not going down that road. I have already spent a lot of time speaking to lawyers to see where I stand on Intellectual property and unfortunately, they said I could spend over 50k on lawyer fees and be unable to prove nothing as Intellectual Property rights can be such a grey area. And because he has so much money than me, he would more likely win the case by employing the best lawyers. I would lose for sure. Only credibility I can take from it is that I should be flattered that either Christopher Nolan or one of his creatives liked my idea- of the SATOR Square being linked with time travel, enough to use it in his blockbuster movie. Or if it is a coincidence of him coming up with the rare idea around the same time, indicates that great minds think alike. Because if the idea was good enough for a world- famous director and arguably the best known director in the world, then my idea was world leading. This is most gratifying to me personally. Given the fact that my copy write was published in 2019 and his movie TENET came out in 2020. I could argue and say I thought of it first having drafted the concept in 2015. It is likely that it would not have taken him 5 years to coincidentally write the concept. Which is why I believe he or one of his colleagues truly seen my work and was inspired by my idea.

14. **I've never seen you talk about your athletic journey. Can you tell me about it?** I always remember my father saying to me after I came 4th in the men's race of a 5-mile road race as a 14-year-old, and he still says now, "Stewy Bell runs against Steve Cram (the world record holder in 1500m at the time) you know." My father was implying that Stewy who won my local town's annual 5-mile road race was a very good runner and I as a junior was not far behind him. I had come 4th man and 1st under 15 boy at age 14 in a time of 26 minutes and 50 seconds, some 3 minutes ahead of the 2nd junior boy. Recently I checked statistics on the athletic website – Power of 10 and compared my result for age with other similar aged junior athletes. The website revealed for my age at 14, my 26 minutes 50 seconds time for 5 miles would

have put me 1st or 2nd in the UK at the time and most likely now. So yes, I know I was national standard at the age of 14. I didn't join a local athletic club as it was too inconvenient to travel to nearest town with a proper track from home town which didn't have one. Which is why I developed as a road runner and cross-country runner more so, racing 5km up to 7-mile distances. I was my own self coach from age 9 to age 15 and influenced, led and motivated my large network of friends into competing at running and athletics at school and outside of school. I would often integrate running as main part of our play whilst playing out, such as; chases, dares, racing competitions, and I even wore ankle weights whilst running as a challenge for my training. I enjoyed running on the roads and the old steelworks grounds with plenty of hills to challenge me. It was just me against the clock. I didn't want competitors to know how I trained. That was my secret. I once turned up for the under 13 regional club Nike run held at Durham city. The distance was 5km. Probably about over 1000 under 13 year old, athletic club runners from about 20 different athletic clubs entered from all over the North East and North of England turned up to race. I ran off into the lead for the first 2km behind a news camera on the back of a van at the front. I faded in the last 2km due to lack of training and came 9th in the end. I was approached by 4 different athletic clubs wanting to sign me as their athlete at the end of the race. There are plenty of other races as a junior which defined my character to run with spirit and drive. Including the time I ran for my school, in a cross-country race. The competitor school marshals deliberately sent us the wrong way, because all 3 of our runners from our school were leading. One of the 3, was me. By the time we found out we had run the wrong way, and turned around to run back, we had found ourselves at the back of the pack. The other 2 runners I was with seemed to mentally give up, as I began to claw myself back up the field of runners. I passed over what seemed about 100 runners in the space of 5 minutes within the woods and ran to the finish line in 5th position. This was the first time I realised I had a double kick. One of my best races as a child aged 13, which demonstrates spirit, determination and physical exhaustion is mentioned in book 3, disguised as a Grazia's memory of personal achievement. This again was a 5km race and was my best demonstration of a double kick as a junior. It also gave me pride that my time for an under 15 was the 5th fastest of all time for 35 years out of approximately 52,500 boys who had ever ran at Holy Island camp over 35 years from 1953 – 1988. I gave up running at the age of 15 sadly, after competing since the age of 9 for school, district, county, and in local road races. My focus at the time diverted to being more interested in attending rave parties as a dancer, at the time.

My achievement of being unbeaten at running in physical education lessons at school over approximately 4 years had come to end. Maybe 100 cross country running sessions over this 4-year period. I remember a first-year boy coming up to me as a 3rd year pupil and saying, "You're the fastest in the school and you're not even in the 5th year." I always knew I still had natural talent, after turning up to a local 5-mile road race at the age of 25 some years later hung over from a drunken night out with old friends, I managed to win the race.

After a Nineteen-year break from training, I took up running again. It was when I entered another 5-mile road race at the age of 34 year and won the race, that I realized I needed to use running as a way of giving me a confidence boost to overcome the adversities of life I was enduring at the time, after being made redundant during the 2008 recession. Running became my saviour, because I was good at it. I began to win the local 5km park runs. I then got scouted by Milton Keynes athletic club to represent them in the 3000m steeplechase and 1500m in the Southern athletic league. I used to run both events on the same day to get points for the club. Shortly after this first season on track, I the represented Milton Keynes in the East of England Veteran league at 800m, 1500m and 3000m. I then represented the East of England at a regional level at 800m and coming 2nd in 1500m, against South of England, West of England, Central England, North of England, Scotland,

Ireland, and Wales.

After a hamstring tendinopathy injury, I diverted to sprinting which would use more of my quadriceps rather than hamstrings. After finding out genetically besides having slow twitch fibres I had fast twitch fibres (which you need for sprinting), as well as possessing good speed technique, this made the decision to switch to sprinting easy for me. I then decided to represent East of England veterans at 4x100m, 200m, 400m and 800m. My biggest accolade as a veteran athlete, is that I am currently the quickest middle distant distance veteran athlete over 40 in the past 50 years at Milton Keynes athletic club, with the quickest 400m time than any other over 40 middle distance veteran athlete. I am proud of my journey and where I have come from as a self-coached junior athlete. It's made me who I am today. A natural born leader, who is strong minded, self-assured, self-disciplined, self-confident, and determined individual.

I have recently overcome 4 years of achilles tendonitis in both legs, and I am currently on track to get back to competing at 800m again as a veteran over 45 years of age.\

15. **At what age did you started writing?** I was always interested in creative writing and won a writing competition at school, at the age of 10. The story was called The Case of the incredible Cornflake - about myself being able to shrink in size when I ate the cereal Cornflakes mixed with sweets. I was able to fly when I shrank in size, after my school friend would kick a football with me sitting on it. A cunning way to escape school without being noticed. Yes, it was from a young age. As I had a very high imagination and would always be called a day dreamer, being caught looking out of the classroom window by teachers. I didn't start seriously writing the trilogy till 7 years ago, but I haven't wrote nonstop through that 7 years. A lot of it has been trying to market the book, redrafting, editing and learning how to self-publish. I would say actually writing the 3 books has took me about 3 years nonstop out of that 7 years including redrafting. But that is also working full time and managing a family. I think I am a natural creative writer, who writes through

influence of own personal endeavors and experience. Hence, I like writing fiction inspired from true events. So I was always destined to be a Dystopian or Sci-Fi writer. But my strong sense of adventure through wanting to empirically experience and demonstrate my own talents in life, has led me to want to write with a sense of suspense, adventure and thriller thread to my writing. Synonymous to my own adventurous journey in life which has been very colourful and illustrious. The fact that I continued to be an academic till the age of 30, having wrote creatively a dissertation for my Bachelor of Arts' first degree and then 2 further Masters of Science degree dissertations. Shows that I have always creatively wrote throughout my life. From the age of 30 till the age of 40 it took my 10 years of realizing I needed to continue to write. From the age of 26 - 40 I had built up 14 years of wind energy and construction industry research as the foundation for some factual information, which I used in my trilogy and it was this wind energy research at a Masters degree level that inspired me to write my trilogy. I think what I was motivated to say, was this. Throughout your life you are constantly soul searching to find what you are good at and what you like, when it can be just glaringly obvious or staring you in your face. All through my life I have creatively wrote, but I just took it for granted.

ACKNOWLEDGMENTS

I would like to sincerely thank Jim Arrowood again for providing his unequivocal support in carrying out the editing for me and a preface which has made me proud to have come across his kind nature and genuineness. Moreover, has made me believe that networking works when you reach out globally into the darkness of the internet and find good people who are caring and helpful. A big thank you goes out to Alishba – also known as the Book Geek as my social media manager, who has been my rock in supporting me and advising me on how to market my book on social media. She has helped me understand it is a long journey and you have to be patient whilst putting hard work in to build up a network of Instagram fans. I owe my fan following and reviews on Instagram to her. I would also like to thank my book formatter Fahadah Madarts, for his persistence in formatting book two and book three.

Thank you to Dr. Philip Barham who again has some contribution in supporting me in writing some of book three. Without his contribution as a ghostwriter, this trilogy would not have been completed. Most of all, thank you to my wife, Jacqueline, and my son, Ethan, for their continued full support, belief, and understanding to help me believe in myself and go the extra mile to complete this third book of the trilogy which again was inspired by current observations and personal experience of contracting the Covid-19 virus a second time within twelve months. Whist the events and characters fortified in the story of book three are fiction, they have been influenced by my own semi-autobiographical research, observations, and experience over the years and currently. The first book was an allegory of capitalism, and corporate and international politics. Whilst this second book is an allegory of leadership, inspired from my own personal leadership experience throughout; my childhood and as an adult, and experience of leadership throughout business and construction. The third book questions what does the future behold for humans, artificial intelligence and the environment. It also questions how our mental health maybe impacted from natural or manmade disasters.

Having lectured and examined leadership and strategy on international MBA courses recently, I have recently practiced as a procurement lead for the national government's UK Health Security Agency on Covid and variant testing.